Something Lovely

By:

Brooke St. James

Other titles available from Brooke St. James:

Another Shot:
(A Modern-Day Ruth and Boaz Story)

When Lightning Strikes

Something of a Storm (All in Good Time #1)
Someone Someday (All in Good Time #2)

Finally My Forever (Meant for Me #1)
Finally My Heart's Desire (Meant for Me #2)
Finally My Happy Ending (Meant for Me #3)

Shot by Cupid's Arrow

Dreams of Us

Meet Me in Myrtle Beach (Hunt Family #1)
Kiss Me in Carolina (Hunt Family #2)
California's Calling (Hunt Family #3)
Back to the Beach (Hunt Family #4)
It's About Time (Hunt Family #5)

Loved Bayou (Martin Family #1)
Dear California (Martin Family #2)
My One Regret (Martin Family #3)
Broken and Beautiful (Martin Family #4)
Back to the Bayou (Martin Family #5)

Almost Christmas

JFK to Dublin (Shower & Shelter Artist Collective #1)
Not Your Average Joe (Shower & Shelter Artist Collective #2)
So Much for Boundaries (Shower & Shelter Artist Collective #3)
Suddenly Starstruck (Shower & Shelter Artist Collective #4)
Love Stung (Shower & Shelter Artist Collective #5)
My American Angel (Shower & Shelter Artist Collective #6)

Summer of '65 (Bishop Family #1)
Jesse's Girl (Bishop Family #2)
Maybe Memphis (Bishop Family #3)
So Happy Together (Bishop Family #4)
My Little Gypsy (Bishop Family #5)
Malibu by Moonlight (Bishop Family #6)
The Harder They Fall (Bishop Family #7)
Come Friday (Bishop Family #8)

Chapter 1

Wes was finally coming home to stay. After spending seven years in London, my big brother was moving back to Memphis. It had been months since I had seen him, and a lot had happened in my life during that time, so I was especially excited for his arrival.

His last trip home had been an eventful one.

He brought a woman with him for the first time since he'd been living in London. Her name was Jolene Wright. She was a real sweetheart who, oddly enough, had mastered the skill of throwing knives. (Leave it to Wes to find someone who looked like the girl next door but knew how to accurately hurl sharp objects across the room.)

As a result of Jolene's influence and her YouTube tutorials, I had taken a liking to knife throwing as well. My dad built a wooden target in the backyard, and I had been using it to practice. I was no Jolene, but I got better and better every time I went out there. It also helped that my dad had bought a nice set of throwing knives. Most of my family had been inspired by Jolene's skills had tried their hand at throwing at the target at least a time or two.

We were all really fond of her. It wasn't just the knife throwing, either. She was a kind, easy-going person who genuinely loved my brother. She fit right in with our family.

It was a good thing we all loved her, because Wes went and married her without telling any of us. They had a secret ceremony the day before they headed back to London, and then they announced it to all of us after the deed had already been done. They had been planning their move back to Memphis ever since. That was six months ago, and today was finally the day.

In fact, I had just gotten a text from my mom saying that Wes and Jolene (along with her family) would be arriving at the house momentarily.

For over two years, I had lived on my own. I had only been back at my parents' house for a couple of months. I didn't own a house or anything, but I did live by myself all that time. My cousin, Shelby, owned a nice little home here in Memphis, and I had been housesitting long-term while she and her family were in Chicago. They had just moved back in November, and now I was back at home with Mom and Dad. While part of me missed my privacy, I had to admit, I enjoyed the home cooked meals and laundry service.

I was standing in the kitchen, but the floorplan in my parents' house was open, so I could see straight through to the living room window, and I knew they had arrived. My parents were driving my mom's SUV, and there was another SUV following right behind them. I knew my dad would drive around to

5

the back of the house and park in the garage, so I walked toward the hallway that would take me out there to meet them.

I wouldn't call it nerves, but I had a sense of anticipation that made me a little jittery, even though it was only my brother. I had already made it out of the house and into the garage by the time my dad parked. The second SUV stopped in the driveway, but I didn't pay much attention to it since I knew my brother was in the one my dad was driving. I could see him.

"I can't believe you're here for good!" was the first thing I said when Wes opened the back door. He was smiling at me, and I scrunched up my face at him. I was so excited he was home.

Jolene was sitting right next to him, and we waved at each other as Wes shifted and stepped out of the vehicle. I hugged him tightly, and he hugged me back.

"Mom said you have big news," he said.

He was right. I did have big news. I had been keeping it from him for the past few months. At first, I didn't mention it because I thought it was too good to be true, but then, once I realized it was really happening, I decided to wait until I could tell him in person.

"I do!" I said. I pulled back, smiling. "Big news," I said with wide eyes.

"We must hear about it," Jolene said as she, too, got out of the backseat.

I reached out to hug her. "It might not be as big of a deal to you," I said, squeezing her neck. "You might not even know who he is."

"I knew it was about a guy," Wes said.

We all shifted to get out of the way as Dad walked toward the back of the SUV to get their luggage.

"Who is it?" Wes asked, looking straight at me. I could tell from the look on his face that he was ready to state his objection. My brothers were all really protective of me. I smiled, knowing that he would most assuredly approve this time.

"Just somebody I've had a crush on *my whole life*."

"Who?" he asked.

"Derek Holbrook!" I said.

I thought Wes would smile, but his face shifted to a mask of confusion.

"*The* Derek Holbrook?" he asked. "The guy who went to Madison?"

I nodded, staring back at him with a similar look of confusion. After all, what *other* Derek Holbrook was there? "Yessss," I said slowly, since that was obvious.

"He's Owen's age," Wes said. His tone was laced with disapproval, and I just regarded him with a disbelieving expression.

"So?" I said. "I thought you'd be excited."

He shook his head a little. "I mean, it's cool, but he's older, Ivy, and he's..." He hesitated, glancing at his wife who was standing next to him, listening to our exchange. "He plays baseball," Wes explained. "He was a big deal when we were in high school."

"He *still is* a big deal," I said. "He plays for the Indians."

"Is that Cincinnati?" Jolene asked hesitantly, like she was really trying to remember.

"Cleveland," I said, smiling at her for getting relatively close. I always thought of her as being from London. I kept forgetting that she was raised here in the U.S. and might know a thing or two about baseball.

"That's so cool," Jolene said, smiling and nodding. "What position does he play?"

"Shortstop," Wes said.

But at the same time, I said, "Second base." I glanced at Wes, shaking my head. "He played shortstop in high school, but he switched over to second a long time ago. He's played second for years." I looked at Jolene. "He was drafted right out of high school. He played for the Mets before he got traded to Cleveland."

"How cooool!" she said.

Again, we were interrupted by my dad who was now walking by, carrying luggage.

"You need help?" Wes asked.

Dad shook his head, letting Wes know he had it under control.

I turned to find that someone else was in Dad's wake, and I knew our conversation about Derek was over—at least for now. I smiled at the man who was walking behind my dad. I assumed it was Mr. Wright, Jolene's dad. I had seen a picture of him, but in the picture, he wasn't sporting a handlebar mustache like he had now, and I studied him, trying to make sure it was the same guy.

"Ivy, this is my dad," Jolene said, confirming my suspicion.

"Ben Wright," the man said, smiling and giving me a nod since his hands were extremely full.

"Ivy Bishop," I said, returning his nod. "Can I help you with your things?"

"Thank you, sweetie, but I believe we've got it under control," he said, still following my dad into the house.

I looked at the second vehicle, the one that was parked in the driveway. My mother was standing near the back of it with two other people who I knew to be Jolene's mom and brother.

I glanced at my brother. "Do y'all need help with anything?" I asked, motioning to the SUV.

He shook his head as he moved to stand behind his wife wrapping his arms around her shoulders. "Nope," he said with a sigh. "We already brought our things by the house on Myrtle."

(My brother, Owen, and his wife, Darcy, owned a ton of rental property, including a house on Myrtle that Wes and Jolene would rent from them for a while until they found a place they liked enough to purchase. It wasn't huge or extravagant, but it was a nice home. We had gotten it somewhat prepared for their arrival with enough furniture to get by and a bed in the master bedroom. They weren't, however, set up to accommodate guests. (It was for this reason that Jolene's family would be staying with my parents this week.)

"How did you like the house?" I asked.

"It's really nice," Jolene said. "Darcy had sent us some pictures, so I knew what to expect, but I liked it even better in person. It's bigger than I thought it was. I can't believe how much work you all put into getting it ready for us."

"The fridge was even full," Wes said.

I smiled and shook my head. "You know Mom."

We started to walk inside, but I glanced over my shoulder at the group who was still outside.

"Do they need help?" I asked.

Wes shook his head. "They packed pretty light. I think Dad and Mr. Wright got most of it."

He and Jolene continued to walk toward the door, but I hesitated. Hospitality was something my mother and grandmothers had engrained in me from a very early age, and I just didn't feel right about heading inside without first greeting the rest of Jolene's family. Sure, I would see them within minutes once they made their way into the house, but that didn't seem good enough. I just couldn't stop myself from going out there to welcome them.

"I'll catch up with y'all inside," I said, speaking to my brother and Jolene from over my shoulder as I turned to head toward the driveway. It was chilly out and a gust of cold wind hit me as soon as I stepped out of the garage. I hunkered down, crossing my arms in front of my chest.

"Hey, nice sweatshirt," I yelled as I drew near and saw what Jolene's brother was wearing.

My mom and Jolene's mom were standing there as well, but they had their backs turned to me. Luke was standing where I could see him, and the first thing I noticed was that he was wearing a black hooded sweatshirt with the old-school Bishop Motorcycles logo across the front.

"Thank you," he said, smiling and looking down at his own shirt as I came to stand next to them.

"Burrr!" I said as I reached out to hug Jolene's mom. "What are y'all doing out here?"

"I was just telling Ginger and Luke about the property," Mom said. "Dad and I were talking about your lot when we went by Wes's place earlier."

'My lot' was actually something my parents had bought. It wasn't right next door, but it was close enough to be seen through the woods—especially now since it was the dead of winter. I had no plans to build a house on it quite yet, but my parents had bought it when it came up for sale a couple of years ago, and since I was the only one of their children who was interested in it at the time, they had sort of promised it to me. I knew the statement didn't require a response, so I just nodded and smiled at Jolene's mom before reaching out to hug her.

"You must be Ms. Ginger," I said. "I'm sure you guessed, but I'm Ivy."

I turned and gave Luke a quick squeeze the same way I had done for his mom. He was not at all what I expected. I had seen a picture of him before, but I did not anticipate his stature. The men in my family were tall—all at least six feet—but Luke was even bigger than them. Derek was six-one, and Luke was definitely taller than him.

"I did guess that," Ginger said sweetly as I hugged her son. "We've heard a lot about you, Miss Ivy."

I grinned at her. I assumed that she would have red hair (with her name being Ginger and all) and I smiled inwardly at the fact that her hair wasn't even close to red. It was light brown and naturally curly, with some grey streaks. She had a kind smile and resembled Jolene in so many ways.

I pulled back, glancing up at Luke and trying to see who he favored. I just couldn't get over how large he was. He was at least a foot taller than Jolene's mom, and from what I saw of Jolene's dad, he was quite a bit taller than him as well. Jolene was also a petite person. Luke seemed to tower over the whole family. I instinctually scanned his face. I found myself staring at his mouth. I couldn't stop looking at it. He had one of those mouths where his top lip was larger than his bottom. He had a different skin tone than the rest of them with dark hair, eyes, and facial hair. He looked nothing like his parents or sister. I didn't expect him to be so tall or so handsome, and I was thrown off. That mouth, my goodness. It was so different. Striking, really.

In addition to all this, it was weird seeing him in a Bishop sweatshirt. I knew he worked for the company, but for some reason, it still surprised me to see him wearing that. I had never even seen that exact design on a hoodie, and I caught myself wanting one of my own. All of those thoughts ran through my mind in a matter of seconds.

"Who do you look like?" I asked, staring up at him. Sometimes, I just said what was on my mind. Sometimes, I spoke out of nerves or surprise without fully considering the repercussions of what I was saying. It wasn't something I was proud of, necessarily, and more often than I liked, it got me in trouble. That moment on my driveway was one of those times—it was not one of my proudest moments.

"What do you mean?" Luke asked, touching his own jaw as he considered my question.

"I mean who do you look like? You know, like in your family. I can't tell who you look like. I can see lots of Jolene in your mom, but it doesn't seem like you resemble either of your parents."

"Oh, that's because I'm adopted," Luke said.

He wore a serious expression.

Dread washed over me.

Maybe it wasn't as bad as asking a girl if she was pregnant when she wasn't, but it was still pretty bad.

Could it possibly be true that Luke was adopted? Jolene had never said anything about her brother being adopted.

I smiled in spite of my own embarrassment. "Are you serious?" I asked, hoping and praying that Luke was like my brothers and was teasing me.

He just smiled and gave me an easy-going nod as if he was completely serious.

Chapter 2

"I had to have an emergency hysterectomy after Jolene's birth," Ginger said.

Mortified.

I was absolutely mortified.

I stared blankly at her.

"We knew we wouldn't be able to have any more children, so we started applying for an adoption when she was still a baby. She was fourteen months old when we got Luke."

My heart was beating like a trapped rabbit. I was an outgoing person who often spoke my mind, but it had been a long time since I had put my foot in my mouth to this extent. Had I really asked him *'who he looked like'?* Uhhhh, for Pete's sake.

"I'm really sorry," I said, since there was nothing for me to do but apologize. "Jolene hadn't mentioned that you were, uh…"

"That's because I'm really sensitive about it," Luke said.

I snapped up to look at him with wide eyes, only to find that he was wearing a solemn, reflective expression. He sighed, staring off into space. "I don't like talking about it. I just want to pretend it never happened… I want to feel like they're my real family, you know?"

My heart was about to beat out of my chest. Sheer horror washed over me, and I wished more than anything that I could take back the last three minutes of my life. I glanced at my mom who was staring at Luke with an expression that was as stunned as I felt.

"Luke Preston Wright, don't you torture this poor girl," Ginger said in a motherly tone. She grinned and pushed at her son's shoulder, and I watched as his serious expression slowly morphed into a teasing, mischievous grin.

I squinted at him, taking a deep breath since I hadn't breathed at all in what seemed like forever. He was joking around with me, and I was completely speechless as a result of it. I gawked at him, noticing his playful smile was laced with a slight apology.

"You totally freaked me out," I said weakly. "Were you joking about *everything*?"

Luke saw how very distressed I was, and he let out a little laugh as he reached out to put his arm around my shoulder. He gave me a few reassuring pats as he smiled down at me. Goodness, he must have been at least six-three—he was so much taller than me.

"I really was adopted," he said "But I'm not sensitive about it. I was kidding about that." He gave me one last squeeze around my shoulders before taking a step back.

"He was just teasing you," Ginger said. She reached up and touched her son's back. "He has nothing to be sensitive about. He's as much my son as if I had birthed him myself."

I sighed. "So, he really was adopted?" I asked.

Ginger nodded.

"I'm so sorry," I said.

"Don't be," Luke said. "I'm the one who should be sorry for messing with you."

"I've got three brothers," I said. "I'm used to being messed with."

My mother, who had been silent through the whole exchange, said something about how cold it was outside before she turned and reached into the back of their rented SUV to grab a suitcase.

"Let me have that one," Luke said, reaching out to take it from my mom. It was obviously the heaviest item left. All of the other bags were small, and we all reached in and grabbed everything.

I was still shaken up on the way inside.

Everyone was standing around the kitchen when we walked in. "I showed Ben to Daniel's room," was the first thing my dad said when he saw us. He was talking to my mom because he was looking straight at her. "I thought you wanted them in Daniel's room and Luke in Wes's. Is that right?"

Mom nodded and then turned to look at Ginger and Luke. "I'll show you to your rooms," she said gesturing for them to follow her. We all walked across the kitchen, headed toward the hallway.

"You guys met Ivy," Jolene noted as we walked into the living room.

"We sure did," Ginger said.

Somewhere in the back of my mind, I thought they might say something about the whole adoption debacle. I almost made a joke about it myself just to mention it before they did. I decided to be quiet, however, and I was glad I did because no one said anything.

We came to Daniel's room first, and my mom walked inside. "Ginger, you and Ben will be in here."

"I'll show Luke to Wes's room," I said from the doorway.

My mom gave me a nod. I thought Luke would follow me, but he squeezed behind me and went into Owen's room with our moms. I was a bit confused at first, but then I realized that he was giving his mother her suitcase.

"Do you know where my bag is?" he asked, talking to his mom as he looked around their room.

"I think Jesse had it," my mom said. "I'm sure he already brought it to Wes's room for you."

I stood in the doorway, waiting for Luke. I was carrying a small duffel bag and I lifted it up, asking if it, too, was supposed to stay in this room.

"That's mine," Luke said, making his way toward me. He smiled and held out his hand, offering to take it from me.

"I've got it," I said as I turned to head down the hall. I pointed to a door on the right as I passed it. "That's your bathroom," I said. "Technically, you have to share it with me, but I'm gone all the time, so I won't be in your way too much."

"Where are you gone to?" he asked.

"What?" I asked, turning to look at him from over my shoulder.

"Where do you run off to?" he asked. "Wes and Jolene said you lived with your parents."

"I do," I said. "For now. But I, my boyfriend. He, uh, has a house here in Memphis, and I go over there a lot."

I had made my way into Wes's room as I was tripping over my words, and by the time I finished speaking, I had set Luke's bag on the foot of the bed and turned to face him.

"Where else would he have a house?" he asked with a little smirk.

"Cleveland," I said. "He lives there half the year." I shrugged. "He's in Arizona a little while, too, but he doesn't have a house there. I think he rents."

Luke tilted his head at me as if he was really trying to follow what I was saying and make sense of it.

I smiled and sighed. "He's a baseball player," I said. "He's from here, and he lives here in the off-season, but he's gone from February through October—sometimes longer, if they make the playoffs."

"That's not half of the year," Luke said. "That's most of it."

"I guess it is," I said with a shrug. "It's gonna be my first year to experience him being gone."

"Why? Is this his first year playing?"

"Oh, no, goodness, no, he's played for a long time. This will be his eighth year. It's just that we've only been dating a few months."

Luke gave me a little smile and nodded in understanding. I couldn't help but stare at his mouth. I wasn't doing it to be inappropriate, but I had always been drawn to looking at people's mouths, and Luke's was particularly different and appealing. I was transfixed. His lips were full, and the way his top lip was larger than his bottom gave his whole face such a striking appearance. Also, I just liked him. I naturally felt comfortable around him. I don't know if it was the sweatshirt or if it was because he took the liberty of teasing me, but I felt really at ease around him—like I could just reach out and hug him for no reason. Maybe it was the sweatshirt.

"Where'd you get your sweatshirt?" I asked.

But there had been a little lull in our conversation, and at the exact same time, he asked, "What's his name?"

"My boyfriend? Derek. Derek Holbrook."

He nodded, and pulled at the front of his shirt. "I got it at the Bishop dealership in London," he said. "That's where I work."

"I know," I said. "My dad told me you were some kind of prodigy."

"I don't know about all that," he said with a humble smile. "I'm not sure if that's a word you could use to describe a mechanic. But I do love my job. Your family makes beautiful bikes. It's a pleasure to work on them, really."

"Are you always this humble?" I asked, thinking that he physically looked bolder than his demeanor indicated.

"Probably not," he said with a little shrug. "I'm just excited to be here. I never thought I'd be staying at Jesse Bishop's house."

I let out a little laugh. "You say that like he's famous."

"He *is* famous," he said, looking at me like I was crazy. "And your granddad... forget about it. Icon."

I laughed again. "Did you just call Doozy an *icon*?"

"He is," Luke said. "A legend."

I stared at Luke, half-wondering if he was making fun. But he wasn't. I could tell by his expression. He was truly excited about meeting my family.

I shook my head. "I'm used to people freaking out about meeting Derek or Courtney. They fall all over themselves asking for an autograph when I tell them I'm dating Derek. It's just funny that you're starstruck over meeting my granddad."

"Is your boyfriend famous or something?"

"I already told you he played for the Indians."

21

Luke shrugged. "Just because he plays pro baseball doesn't mean he's famous."

"Well he is," I said. "He's super famous. He's been on the All-Star team for the last three years. He's got a bobble head and everything."

Luke dug in his bag. He wasn't *unimpressed*, but he was definitely less impressed than I wanted him to be. "Michael Bishop should have a bobble head," he said with an amused grin.

Part of me was mad that Luke didn't really care who Derek was, and other part was happy that he loved my family so much. I had such conflicting emotions that I didn't even know what to say.

After digging in his bag for several long seconds, he finally came up with a small stack of pictures. He handed them to me. "These are some pictures from the dealership. We had a little party for Amos's birthday. Al's wife printed them out. Everybody wanted me to bring them with me so I could show your dad and grandpa."

I flipped through the photographs one by one. I had seen a lot of Bishop dealerships in my life. I had basically grown up in one. I did get a surreal feeling flipping through those pictures, however. I thought of this get-together happening all the way over there in London, England. These people shared an undeniable kinship. They were like a big family, and they were all brought together by my grandfather's motorcycle legacy—I could see the motorcycles in the background, and it felt like home to me even though I'd never been there before.

"My dad's gonna love these," I said, staring down at them.

There were maybe twenty or so pictures, and I continued to flip through them. Some of them were posed group shots and others were candid photos of them sitting around, eating birthday cake.

"Who is this?" I asked, holding up a picture for Luke to look at.

"Chasidy," he said.

"Oh, so the girls at the dealership just sit on y'all's laps? That's how y'all do it over there in England?"

"Chasidy's my girlfriend," he said.

"Oh, it was a *girlfriend party*," I said.

I didn't mean for it to be, but my tone was maybe somewhat confused or annoyed, and Luke gave me a slightly funny look on account of that—like he almost wasn't sure if he was supposed to respond to my statement or not. Rather than addressing it directly, he leaned over and pointed at the other picture—the one I was holding in my left hand—the one that was on top of the stack.

"This is Amos's girlfriend, and there's Randall's wife," he said, pointing at two specific women in the photograph. "The party was afterhours, so everyone brought their spouses."

I placed the picture of Luke and Chasidy on top of the stack and stared at it again. She was gorgeous—petite with cute, mouse-like features that made her look innocent and young. She looked like one of my friends at college named Megan, except Megan had black hair where this girl's hair looked to be... "Is she a redhead?" I asked, peering at the photograph.

"It's kinda dark red, but yeah," Luke said. "I think it's naturally more brownish, but she does something to it."

She really was beautiful. I sat there and inspected that picture—staring at her sitting on Luke's lap. Looking at it gave me the oddest sensation. I wouldn't call it jealousy, necessarily, but I felt some type of way when I looked at her—some type of negative way, like I begrudged her for being beautiful, or for where she was sitting, or how she was smiling. I was inexplicably annoyed by this girl, which was the most ridiculous thing ever.

"She's gorgeous," I said to Luke, fighting against my own nonsensical feelings.

"Thank you," he said. "She's studying to be a teacher."

"Oh, really? Me too." I handed him back the stack of photographs. "I should say I might be. I'm not exactly sure what I want to do. I'm studying math. My mom said I could take over her accounting job at the company, but I kinda think I might want to teach. I don't really care about accounting math. I'm more of a straight-up geometry and algebra person. I really do enjoy complicated equations. I know that

24

probably makes me seem like a nerd—I promise I'm not. I just like numbers. I know most people don't. That's why I think it would be rewarding to teach. We've all had that one teacher who inspired us. I'd like to do that for people with math. So many people hate math. Maybe I could try to make it cool, you know?"

I was officially rambling, so I stopped myself and just smiled at him.

"I was never inspired by a teacher," Luke said, staring at the wall as if really trying to remember a time.

"You weren't? Not even one?"

He shook his head. "I mean, I know those kinds of teachers exist—I think my dad might be one of them. He's really well-loved by his students. Don't get me wrong, I had some teachers I liked—some that I thought were good instructors who were good at their jobs, but no. There was no one who I would say *inspired me*. I think it's just gotta be the right student who lines up with the right teacher. It's a two-way street. I'm sure if my school would've offered a class on building motorcycles it would have been a different story."

Chapter 3

Luke and I were still standing in Wes's room, having a conversation when some movement in the hallway caught our attention. We both turned to look in that direction.

It was my mom. She had peered around the doorframe and was standing there, smiling at us. "Just checking on y'all," she said. "We're gonna order pizza for dinner. I'm going to call to place an order in just a minute. Luke, do you have any special requests?"

"I eat anything," he said with a smile.

"Is anyone coming over?" I asked.

Mom shook her head. "No. I'm cooking for everybody tomorrow night, but I thought we'd just lay low and get some take-out tonight—just us. I didn't want to overwhelm these guys on their first day."

"We don't mind," Luke said. "You guys should just do what you normally do."

"We are," Mom said, smiling. "Pizza's normal. I know y'all have had a long day of traveling. We'll have the rest of the family over tomorrow, after you've had the chance to relax a little bit."

"Derek will probably eat with us," I said. "He's coming over to pick me up in a little bit."

"I figured he would," Mom said, with a smirk. "I'm surprised Britney's not coming, too." She winked at Luke. "I have to plan for one or two extras with this one, even if we're *not having anybody over.*"

Mentioning Derek made me remember the conversation I had with Luke and how much of a fan he was of my grandfather. "Luke's excited to meet Doozy," I said to Mom.

"Doozy's excited to meet him, too," Mom said. "Everybody's heard about how talented you are."

"Thank you," Luke said. "I was telling Ivy... it's a real honor to meet all of you. I'm such a fan of your motorcycles. I just love Mister Bishop's style."

"Oh, Doozy's gonna looove talking shop with you," Mom said.

"I'm looking forward to it," Luke replied.

Mom smiled before disappearing into the hallway again.

Luke sighed. "It's surreal being here," he said.

"Why? Because my granddad builds motorcycles?"

"You say it like he's not a legend," Luke said.

"It would be like if you got to go spend the night at some famous mathematician's house, like..." he hesitated as if searching his brain for the name of a mathematician. "I'm sure there are famous mathematicians, right?"

I smiled. "Einstein. Newton."

"Yeah," he said "It would be like if you got to spend the week at Einstein's house."

"You're as big of a nerd as I am. You're just a motorcycle nerd, and I'm a math nerd."

"You're not a nerd," he said, shaking his head a little. "Nerd is not even close to the word I would use to describe you."

"What's the word you'd use?"

"I don't know. Not nerd, that's for sure. You're smart, but that doesn't mean you're a nerd."

"What if I told you I love to read?" I asked.

He shrugged. "That just goes along with you being smart," he said. "It still doesn't make you a nerd. It's weird that you even use that word about yourself. It's just about the *last* word I would ever use to describe you."

I held my palms up as if asking him to evaluate my appearance. I even shifted a little, letting him get a good look. "What word would you use to describe me then?"

He hesitated, staring at me—his dark eyes regarding me seriously. "Do you just need to hear that you're beautiful?" he asked, surprising me.

"No," I said with a scowl. "Why would you say that?"

"Because that's the only word to describe you—I mean, if I'm going on looks. I could say stunning, or gorgeous, or lovely, or pretty, but they all mean the same thing, really. Beautiful. You're a beautiful woman, Ivy. Obviously. You must know that. Regardless of whether or not you're a Bishop, bobble head baseball players don't just go around dating any-old, homely-old girl."

I had to smile at his statement. It was funny to me that he referred to Derek as a 'bobble head baseball player'.

"Well, I wasn't fishing for a compliment, but thank you. I'm glad to know you don't think I'm a homely-old girl."

He gave me a confident smirk as he shook his head. "I'm sure you were really torn up, waiting for my opinion, wondering what I thought."

"I *was* wondering," I said, seriously. "You're acting like I was joking around, but I wasn't. I really wanted to know how you'd describe me—what you thought of me."

"You're beautiful," he said. "Breathtakingly beautiful. That's the first thing I noticed when I saw you. Then you spoke, and I realized you were so much more than that. You have it on the inside, too. I loved that you blushed and got all embarrassed the very first time we met. It made me feel like you didn't mind putting yourself out there—it made me feel welcome."

I was blushing again as he spoke—I could feel my face getting hot. "You're making me shy over here," I said, fanning my face. "And I don't normally get shy. Usually, I'm the one being all honest and straight-forward. I'm not used to meeting someone else who does that."

"I'm sorry," he said. "I'm just telling you how I see it. You can't call yourself a nerd just because you like math and reading."

The truth was, I didn't really see myself as a nerd at all. I just said that to be funny, mostly. I was pretty confident in my non-geekness. My parents and family had always been really supportive about my academic endeavors, and no one ever gave me a hard time about studying math or having my nose in a book.

I hadn't expected Luke to be so sincere and earnest in his response, though, and I replayed his words in my mind. He said I was beautiful inside and out, and he truly meant it—all this sincerity from a guy I had just met. I really thought I had blown the first impression with Luke and his mom, and I was relieved that he saw it differently.

"You're unbelievably nice," I said.

He shrugged casually. "I'm just speaking the truth."

Before I knew what was happening, he stepped around me, walked past me, and headed for the hallway.

"Where you going?" I asked.

"I thought we'd go out here with everyone else," he said.

"Oh, yeah, of course."

I followed Luke down the hall. I thought he would stand back and let me lead the way since it was his first time at the house, but he wasn't timid at all. He just assumed I would follow him, which I did.

"Dad said you've been practicing your knife throwing skills." I heard Wes's statement as soon as Luke rounded the corner. Apparently, my brother thought I would be coming out first because he was talking to me when he said that.

"I have," Luke said, knowing full-well that Wes's statement wasn't meant for him. "Chasidy wanted to learn how to do it, so I've been getting my chops together so I can teach her." We had both come into the living room by that point, and he glanced back at me with a smile. "But I think he was talking to you," he said. "Have you been practicing, too?"

"I have," I said.

Everyone besides my mother was sitting around the living room on couches and chairs, and Luke and I went in there to join them. He sat on the big sectional with Wes, Jolene, and his parents, and I took a seat on an ottoman near my dad, who was sitting in an armchair.

"Dad built a target in the backyard, and I've been trying it out a little bit. I've been using Jolene's YouTube videos for instruction, but I think I'll do better now that she's here." I glanced at Jolene. "Speaking of... did Dad tell you about Uncle Gray wanting to hire you?"

"I didn't want to bombard her," Dad said. "I was gonna give her a day to settle in before we start trying to put her to work all over town."

"Does he need graphic design work?" Jolene asked since that was what she had done professionally in London.

"We all need that," Dad said, talking about the Bishop company. "And Gray might need it at Alpha, too, but he was thinking about asking you to teach a few classes on knife throwing—you know, to the guys."

Jolene glanced at her parents, who were sitting at the end of the couch, listening to the conversation. "Did I tell you about Wes's uncle?" she asked.

"The one that has a bodyguard company?" Ginger asked.

Jolene nodded.

"It's called Alpha Security," Wes said. "Uncle Gray is ex-military—a lot of his guys are. He's got a pretty intense training facility. They provide personal security to anyone who's in the market for that kind of thing—musicians, presidents, the pope. He's got guys working all over the world. My oldest brother, Daniel, works for him. That's how he met Courtney."

Jolene's parents must have been aware that our brother was married to the pop star, Courtney Cole, because they nodded in understanding when Wes made that statement.

"Gray's got a two-year program," Dad explained. "The guys live right there on site. He trains them with weapons, martial arts, all kinds of stuff. He said they know how to use a knife, but he's never done an actual class on knife throwing."

"Oh, Jolene would be perfect for that," Ben said.

"Okay, the pizza's ordered!" Mom called, coming into the room from the hallway on the other side of the kitchen and not hearing anything we were saying.

"Do you need us to go pick it up?" Ginger asked.

"Oh, no, they're delivering it," Mom said. "They said it would be here within the hour."

She crossed the room and, without hesitation, sat in the chair with my father. He shifted around, making room for her and then held on to her by the waist like they were a couple of teenagers.

"I think it'd be fun," Jolene said, smiling at my dad.

"What would?" Mom asked, glancing at Dad.

"We were telling her about Gray wanting to hire her to work with the guys."

"Oh, good," Mom said, nodding.

"I know he's Wes's uncle," Luke said. "But how are you guys related again?"

"I've got a twin sister named Jane," Dad explained. "She's married to Gray, and they own the security business."

"There's a lot of you to keep straight," Luke said.

33

My dad laughed. "Rose and I have four kids, and Jane and Grey have two. Between our kids and the grandbabies coming along, it seems like we're celebrating a birthday every time we turn around. Rose has brothers who live in town, too. One or two of them will probably be here tomorrow night. You'll meet so many people that you won't be able to keep names straight."

"That's so neat," Ginger said. "We don't know what it's like to have a big family. Ben's an only child. I have a sister in Atlanta who has two grown kids, but we rarely have the chance to get together—especially since we moved to London."

"Did you ever think about moving back?" I asked.

Ginger smiled at me. "We think about it all the time," she said. "Even more now that Jolene's moving back." She paused and glanced at Mr. Wright with a little smile and shrug. "We kind of go where the wind blows," she said. "Ben's always wanted to live in Europe. There's so much rich history over there—such great art. He's had the opportunity to see so much of it since we've been there. He's traveled all over Europe, checking out museums. There are just so many classics."

"I've even seen a couple of private collections that might as well be museums," Ben added.

"You're a full-time professor, right?" Dad asked.

Ben nodded. "I took a sabbatical two years ago and did nothing but travel and do research for six months. Ginger came with me for a lot of it. It was amazing. There's so much art over there."

"And that's what you teach?" Dad asked. "Art?"

"Art History."

"Oh, how perfect," Mom said.

Ben nodded. "I was in Amsterdam when I saw a Vermeer painting called The Milkmaid. It's just so beautiful. Really amazing. I had seen it in pictures lots of times, but it was a different experience to come face-to-face with it. I remembered seeing this documentary that speculated how Vermeer might have used a gadget to do his art, and seeing that painting in person set me off on this whole mission to try to do it myself—recreate it the same way the guy in the documentary did. That's been quite a project."

"Wes and Jolene were telling us a little bit about that," Mom said.

"I've seen that documentary," I said. "We watched it in an art class I took a few years ago. It was really cool. I'm not even into that kind of thing, and I remember wanting to try it myself."

Ben smiled and nodded at me, lifting his eyebrows like he had been having lots of fun with it.

"Did you do it?" I asked.

He continued to nod.

"Did it work?"

"Pretty much," he said with a shrug. "I don't know if I'd call it a Vermeer, but it came out pretty close. It's definitely better than anything I could have done on my own."

"It's really awesome," Luke said. "They both did a great job."

"My mom had to sit there and model like that lady for I don't know how many hours." Jolene added.

"Weeks," Ginger said, laughing. "Months even."

"She was a real trooper," Ben said. "She had to stand there and hold this pitcher for hours at a time. We had to build a contraption to help her hold it up so her arms didn't give out."

Ginger flexed her muscles. "I've got biceps for days after that experience," she said, causing us all to laugh.

"I wish we could see it," Mom said.

Ben got up from his place on the couch. "I've got some pictures in my suitcase."

Chapter 4

"Luke's got some pictures, too," I said.

Luke glanced at me, and I smiled.

"The ones you showed me of Amos's birthday," I said, even though he knew full-well what I was talking about. I knew he was still a little intimidated about meeting my dad and wasn't planning on breaking out the pictures just yet, but he was sweet, and I couldn't help but put him on the spot a little. Honestly, it was neat for me to experience someone being starstruck over my father. I was used to seeing people freak out over meeting Courtney, and in recent months, I had seen my fair share of people come unglued over meeting Derek, but I had rarely, if ever, met someone who truly appreciated the work of my father and grandfather the way Luke did.

"I'll show him sometime," Luke said casually.

"Just go get them," I said. "He'll love seeing them." I glanced over my shoulder at my dad. "Luke brought some pictures of the guys at the London dealership," I said.

"Oh, please go get them," Mom said. "Jesse and Doozy have been wanting to make it over there to see that location. We'd love to see your photos."

Luke stood up and headed toward the bedroom to get his photos. Mr. Wright left the room before Luke, so he beat him back, carrying the photos of the painting. I had been expecting just a few photographs of the finished project, but he brought a stack of at least thirty pictures, documenting the whole process. We passed around the stacks of pictures, asking Ben questions about his painting and asking Luke questions about his job.

Ben Wright was an extremely nice man, but I couldn't help but notice that he wasn't overly excited about Luke working at a motorcycle shop. He had manners about it, and he didn't say anything offensive to Luke or to my father, but a few of the comments he made led me to believe that he thought Luke's current job situation was temporary.

Maybe I was just protective of Luke because he was kind and charming, or maybe I had a soft spot for motorcycles in general, but either way, I was sensitive to every little nuance in Ben's tone, and I couldn't help but conclude that he thought Luke was capable of doing more with his life. It could be that I was just over analyzing it, though, and I told myself that.

I looked at Luke's photos again even though I had seen them in the bedroom. Everybody seemed happy at the dealership. When I came to the one of Luke with Chasidy on his lap, I realized it still gave me odd feelings. Normally, I enjoyed seeing other people happy, but that girl just annoyed me. I knew those feelings were totally uncalled for, so I quickly shifted the picture to the back of the stack and looked at a few others to get a different image in my head. I was still flipping through them when I felt my phone vibrate in my pocket.

I leaned over, stretching out to hand the stack to my brother before taking my phone out of my pocket. Derek was supposed to be at my house any minute, so I assumed the text would be from him, but instead, it was from my friend, Britney.

Britney: "What are you up to?"

I typed out a text to her.

Me: "About to eat with the fam. Derek's coming over. We're hanging at his house tonight."

Britney: "What are y'all eating?"

This was a question I had heard from Britney hundreds of times over the years. She and I had been friends since we were kids, and she had eaten countless meals at our house. Seriously. Countless. Britney didn't have the best home life. She wasn't abused or anything, but her parents didn't have much money, and they didn't really care about cooking meals and eating them as a family.

She had an older sister that was already out of the house by the time we were in middle school, so it was really just her and her parents, and they weren't necessarily stand-up individuals. She went to college on a cheerleading scholarship and moved into the dorms, although a lot of nights she just stayed with me at Shelby's house rather than in her dorm room. To say she had eaten a lot of meals with my family over the years would be an understatement.

I texted her back, knowing that once I told her we were eating pizza, she'd ask if she could come over. She loved pizza—especially from Mama Carlotta's.

Me: "Pizza. Jolene and Wes got here today. Jo's parents are here."

Britney: "I forgot they were coming home today. That's awesome. I bet Rose is in heaven. Do y'all care if I come by for pizza? I won't stay. I have nothing in my fridge."

Me: "Come on."

Britney: "Is it Mama Carlotta's?"

Me: "Yep."

Britney: "Yasssss!!!!! Be there in 20."

I tossed my phone onto the ottoman next to me. "Britney's coming over for pizza," I said.

Mom nodded as if this news didn't surprise her at all. "I thought Derek was coming, too."

"He is. He'll be here any—" I trailed off because I saw the reflected light coming through the window as his truck pulled into the driveway. I got a giddy feeling in the pit of my stomach that caused a smile to spread across my face.

I had a crush on him for so many years. He was older than me, and he was a local sports hero, so for what seemed like all of my adolescence, Derek Holbrook was basically unobtainable. We had been dating exclusively for three months, and I still felt like I had to pinch myself when he came around.

I popped up from my seat, jogging across the living room and kitchen so that I could go outside and meet him.

"Who's here?" Derek asked, pointing at Jolene's parents' rental as he climbed out of his truck.

I smiled at the sight of him. He was tall and thick with the build of a professional athlete. He had on stylish, athletic clothes and a pair of tennis shoes that had not a single scuff on them—I swear he wore a new pair every day.

"Wes got back today," I said, smiling at the smell of his cologne as he hugged me. "Jolene's family is here, too. They came to meet us and help her get settled."

Derek looked toward the house even though he couldn't see anyone from where we were standing. "Are they nice?" he asked.

I nodded.

"Are they British?"

I shook my head. "They're from America. They've just been living in England."

"How long are they gonna be here?"

"Four or five days."

"Why don't you just sleep at my house?" he asked.

I smiled and squinted at him. It was definitely tempting, but I couldn't do it. Derek was insatiable, and I knew we would get in trouble if I stayed the night there.

We walked in together, and I felt an undeniable sense of pride as I introduced him to Wes, Jolene, and her family. He was handsome with Southern charm, and he had the confidence of a man who had, for the last few seasons, been one of the MLB's most valuable players.

During the introduction, my mom informed Jolene's parents that Derek played pro baseball.

"Ben used to be a big baseball fan when we lived in the States," Ginger said.

"Oh, really?" Derek asked cordially.

"The Phillies," Ben said. "We lived in Philadelphia way back in the Mike Schmidt days. I used to love to go to the games. Even after we moved to Georgia, I used to keep up with the Phillies."

"We devastated the Phillies last year," Derek said.

His statement took us off guard and we all sort of looked at him with awkward, wide-eyed glances.

Derek's face broke into a confident grin. "I'm just kiddin', they swept us."

Ben, who hadn't been expecting to meet a baseball player, let alone get teased by one, let out a hearty laugh at Derek's joke. "You had me on that one," he said.

Derek smiled as he sat on the ottoman next to me. "Philly had a solid team last year," he said.

"What position do you play?" Ben asked.

"Second base." He looked at my brother, who had stood to shake his hand, but was now sitting on the couch next to Jolene. "I played against this guy a time or two," Derek said.

"Back in the day," Wes said.

"Ivy said you were doing music now."

Wes nodded.

"Singer-songwriter or what?" Derek asked.

"Pretty much," Wes said. "Maybe not as folky as that phrase makes it sound, but yeah, I write songs."

"What'd your band think about you leaving?" Derek asked.

"They weren't too excited about it," Wes answered with a shrug. "But what are you gonna do? Life goes on, I guess."

Derek nodded. "Same with me, with people getting traded and stuff. You make relationships, and it's hard to leave, but it's part of the job."

Wes nodded.

"Ivy took me by the house y'all are renting," Derek added. "It's not too far from mine. I'll have to have you over sometime soon. We could watch some football."

"Sounds good," Wes said.

Derek was the type who liked to keep the conversation going. He was like me in that he was somewhat restless and liked to make sure that there was continual action and that no one got bored. That's why it didn't surprise me that he was doing a lot of the talking. He turned his attention to Luke, who had been quietly observing the conversation. "So, you're Jolene's brother?" he asked.

Luke nodded. "I am."

"Older?" Derek asked.

"Younger," Luke said.

"What do you do?"

"I'm a mechanic," Luke said.

He was not at all embarrassed to say that. On the contrary, he was quite calm and confident.

Ben, on the other hand, let out a nervous laugh. "He's working with motorcycles, on motorcycles, repairing them and rebuilding them." he explained. "He's got a job at the Bishop dealership in London for now. That's how Wes and Jolene met."

"It's not just for now," Luke said, shaking his head a little and correcting his father in the most calm, respectful way possible. "I really love my job. I hope to get into designing and building."

"You mean motorcycles?" Derek asked. "You want to design and build *motorcycles*?"

Luke nodded, and Derek turned to glance at my father. "I think you're probably in the right house for that," he said.

"I think you're probably right," Luke said. "I'm hoping it's something in the water, or Mrs. Bishop's cooking—I'm trying to soak it all in while I'm here."

"Randall said you're really talented," Jesse said. "He said you had some designs of your own."

"I do," Luke said.

"We've got another young man at our Los Angeles location who shows promise as a designer, and one in Miami, I believe. Dad and I were talking about having a contest of sorts… maybe let anyone who wants to enter submit a design, and the winner would get their bike built in the new line."

Luke sat on the edge of the couch, looking at my dad with an earnest expression. "That would be amazing," Luke said. "Would you really think of doing that?"

"Would you enter?" Dad asked.

"Definitely," Luke said. "Could you enter more than one design?"

"I don't see why not," Dad said, smiling at his enthusiasm. "We were thinking we'd judge it blind—you know, so it'd be fair."

"Of course," Luke said.

"How many do you think you'd enter?"

Luke shook his head. "Is there a limit?"

That question caused my dad to laugh. "Well, there's no contest yet, but I guess there wouldn't be a limit—especially since we wouldn't know who did what. There's still a lot to figure out. We'd have to provide the same templates for everyone."

"Maybe you could scribble your initials in the corner since you know the family now," Derek said. We all looked at him, and he smiled and winked at Luke.

"I wouldn't want any favors," Luke said. "I'm about to win this thing fair and square."

Derek laughed at that—not in a demeaning way, but more in an appreciative way. As a competitor, he could completely understand Luke's drive, and I could tell by the way he smiled at Luke that he liked him.

"Do you ride?" Ginger's question was directed to Derek, but I pretended to think she was talking to me. I was so psyched about Luke's love for motorcycles that I couldn't help myself. I wanted his parents to appreciate how cool they were.

"Yes ma'am, I've been riding since I was little. I got my first bike before my first car."

"I don't," Derek said, knowing she'd been talking to him. "I mean, I could. I'm sure I know how to do it. I rode a little when I was younger, but I don't anymore. I know it sounds silly, but it's in my contract that I can't."

"Oh, you mean for safety?" Ginger asked.

Derek nodded. "No motorcycles, no skydiving… I have a few things that are off limits. My trainers don't even like me playing backyard ball."

"That makes sense," Ben said.

We were still talking about baseball and motorcycles a few minutes later when Britney pulled into the driveway.

46

Chapter 5

Britney knocked a couple of times, but she could see us all sitting in the living room, so she just walked right in without anyone getting up to answer the door. She came in wearing a huge, charismatic smile as usual.

Wes and Jolene both stood up to greet her, and Jolene's family followed suit. "Who's this?" Britney asked after she hugged Wes.

"This is my brother, Luke," Jolene said. "And my parents, Ben and Ginger."

"I didn't know you were bringing your brother," Britney said.

She stepped closer to Luke. He held out his hand to shake hers, and she denied him with a smile, going for the hug instead. "Cool sweatshirt," she said, pinching at it.

"Thanks," he said.

She moved on down the line, offering quick but sincere Southern-style hugs to everyone else in line, first Ginger and then Ben. My parents, along with Derek and me remained in our seats.

"These are my parents, Jesse and Rose," I said, messing with her.

She bowed to them. "I'm pleased to make your acquaintance," she said, smirking. "Ivy said we're having Mama Carlotta's for dinner," she added as she plopped onto the couch.

This made everyone laugh.

"I called Kade on my way over here," she said. "He said he's delivering it. He should be here in just a minute. He had one other stop to make."

"I thought Kade was in Nashville," I said.

Britney shook her head. "He came back early. He picked up a shift tonight because somebody was sick. He said he tried to call you earlier."

I nodded absentmindedly, thinking about seeing Kade's name in my missed calls. "You know how I am with my phone," I said. "I saw that he called, but I forgot."

Kade was another one of my good friends. I wasn't as tight with him as I was with Britney, obviously, but we were really close friends and had been for years. We all went to high school and then to college together. He had been raised going to my granddad's church, so we went way back. Also, he was majoring in biology, so we had some classes together in college. He was a smart guy who was working his way through college by delivering pizzas at Mama Carlotta's.

He was also a good person. In fact, his recent trip to Nashville was for a retreat with the church youth group. Everyone told me over the years that Kade was hopelessly in love with me, but I just didn't see it. It wasn't like that with us. We were good friends and that was all. He had never even mentioned having feelings for me, and I certainly didn't have any for him—at least not the romantic kind.

"Kade's a friend of Ivy's," Mom said, explaining our conversation to the Wrights. "He's a real sweet guy. They've been friends a long time."

"Speak of the d, d, dickens..." Britney said, looking out the window.

Kade had just pulled into the driveway, and Britney was about to say *speak of the devil*, but she caught herself, and knowing that my mom wouldn't want her to refer to Kade as 'the devil', she changed her statement at the last second.

"Speak of the *dickens*?" Wes asked, looking confused, and giving Britney a hard time. "What's that mean?"

"Speak of the *angel*," Dad said, teasing Mom.

No one else really understood what was being said, but they didn't have to—no one cared or was even listening. Mom stood up, and everyone began to follow her lead, getting up to go to the kitchen or otherwise prepare to eat dinner.

My dad went to answer the door while Derek and I went to the kitchen along with most of the others. He stayed close to me, touching me in some way at all times—either holding my hand or simply standing close enough for our shoulders to touch.

Dad and Kade walked into the kitchen together, and Kade's eyes widened. "I knew you had company by how many pies you ordered," he said. "I thought maybe Daniel and Owen would be here."

"It's the other brother," Wes said, coming into the kitchen.

"Kade turned, regarding Wes with an excited smile. "When'd you get here?" he asked.

"A little while ago," Wes said.

Kade reached out to give him a sideways hug. "Welcome home," he said. "Are these the in-laws?"

Wes nodded. "You met Jolene, didn't you?"

"We did, the last time you were here," Kade said, shaking Jolene's hand.

Kade and Dad had already set the thermal pizza bags on the counter, and my mom was helping herself to everything that was inside. I went over there to help her as Wes continued introducing Kade to Jolene's family.

"Are you going to eat with us?" Mom asked Kade during a break in their conversation.

"No ma'am. Thank you, but I already ate," Kade said. "I'll stay and hang out for a few minutes, though."

He leaned against the counter in a spot nearby Derek, and I watched out of the corner of my eye as they made a little small talk. Mom and I were busy opening pizza boxes and setting everything out while everyone else stood around the kitchen and talked amongst themselves, all making an effort to stay out of the way.

Britney cozied up next to Luke. I noticed it right when she went over there. She was a little bit of a flirt, and I was used to that. Usually, it didn't bother me, but for some reason, I wanted to take up for the girl in the picture in spite of the fact that I really didn't like her in the first place. I wanted to announce to Britney, right there in front of everyone, that Luke had a girlfriend and thus was off-limits. I kept cutting my eyes at them, but they didn't even notice me.

"Britney, here's your favorite," I announced, opening a box that contained a Tuscan Chicken pizza. I was trying to distract them, but it didn't really work.

Kade had to be getting back to work, so he only stayed a few minutes. The rest of us hung out at the house for the next hour or so, eating and talking about everything under the sun from music, to baseball, to motorcycles, to art, to math. Sometimes we would talk to the person next to us, and other times a conversation would take over the whole room.

Toward the end of dinner, the conversation turned to knife throwing. My dad announced to everyone that I had been practicing quite a bit, and they all wanted to see me show my skills. I declined, saying that it was too cold outside and that Derek and I already had plans and needed to be going. I promised I would do it sometime soon, but I kind of hoped it didn't get brought up again—at least not while Jolene's family was still visiting. I had gotten a lot better at it since I'd been practicing, but I knew they were all good at it, so I wasn't in a hurry to stand there and try it in front of all of them.

"We're gonna go," I said once we were done with dinner. Everyone was in the living room, but I had just gone into the kitchen with Mom and Wes.

"Why are you running off?" Wes asked.

I shrugged. "Derek and I had plans to hang out."

"You can hang out here," Wes said, drawing a smile from our mom.

"You and Jo are gonna be going to your place, anyway," I said.

Wes shook his head. "Not right this second."

"She likes to go to Derek's house," Mom said. She rolled her eyes. "He's got a hot tub."

"You don't need to be in a hot tub with that dude," Wes said.

I glanced into the living room just to make sure Derek hadn't overheard, but he was nowhere in sight. He had gone to the restroom and hadn't come back yet.

I smirked at Wes. "Says the guy who went gallivanting around London for seven years."

"I still don't want my little sister in a hot tub with that dude. I see how he looks at you, Ivy."

"He looks at me like I'm his girlfriend. And stop calling him dude. His name is Derek, Wes. You know him. I thought you'd be happy for me that I finally found a guy I really like."

"I don't really know him, though. And I can't tell if I like him. You just think he's all that because he's famous. Have Owen and Daniel met him? Do they like him?"

"Why are you being so crabby?" I asked. My serious expression broke into an overly patient, fake grin. "Is it that no one's good enough for your little sister?"

"No, it's just that *he's* not good enough."

I glanced into the living room. Derek had just come out of the bathroom and was standing there smiling and making pleasant conversation with my dad. I pointed at him with a completely confused expression aimed at my brother. "I have no idea what you're talking about," I said. "He's really nice."

"He's just protective of you," Mom said, standing next to Wes and rubbing his back as if she was taking up for him.

I turned my confused expression to her. "I don't need to be protected. I happen to be dating the most eligible bachelor in Memphis. And he's sweet. He's a nice guy. Your trippin', Wes."

Wes shook his head and gave me a shrug that looked somewhat frustrated. "Whatever, Ivy. Just please be careful."

"I will. And I love you. Welcome home."

I glanced toward the living room to find that Derek was now walking toward me wearing a smile.

"I love you, too," Wes said. He had been sitting on a stool, and he sighed as he stood up.

"You ready?" Derek asked, still smiling at me.

I nodded.

Wes headed into the living room, looking like he was going to trade places with Derek. They were standing only a few feet from me when they crossed paths, and I watched them smile and shake hands cordially.

"It was nice seeing you again," Wes said.

"Same here," Derek said. "I know Ivy's glad you moved home. We'll have to get together sometime before I head to Arizona."

Wes nodded. "Sounds good."

Within minutes, I had gathered my things and told everyone goodbye.

Britney was sitting on the couch. It appeared as if she was planning on staying in spite of my departure. I had to literally ask her if she was coming when we headed out. She took her time getting her shoes on at the door, so Derek walked out ahead of us, saying that he was going to get the truck warmed up.

"I feel bad for Luke," Britney whispered as she put on her shoes. I knew she was thinking about Luke, and I felt a wave of annoyance and cynicism about it.

"Why?" I asked.

"Because he doesn't have anybody to hang out with. He's just got to sit here and hang out with your parents and his parents."

I gave her a disbelieving expression as I gestured toward the living room. "Wes and Jolene are here," I said. "Luke's fine."

She snickered. "You can say that again."

"What?" I asked, feeling confused.

"You said *'Luke's fine'*, and I said 'you can say that again'. He's fine. He looks good. Get it?"

She was being playful and lighthearted, and I just felt annoyed.

"He's got a girlfriend," I said.

"Yeah, but she's all the way over in London."

"What's that supposed to mean? You want him to cheat on her just because you're here and she's not?"

Britney made a cautious face at me as if I was a bomb that was about to explode. "Noooo," she said like I was way overreacting. "It means that he doesn't have anyone to hang out with, that's all."

"He's got his sister, and Wes, and our families. He's fine."

She smiled. "I'm not going to take the bait and joke about how *fine* he is again, because I see how worked up you are over it." She gestured by waving her hand in my general direction as if to imply that I was really shaken up.

"I'm not worked up," I said.

"So, you can admit that he's hot."

"I don't need to admit that. There's no point."

"You can at least appreciate a hot guy when you see one, can't you?"

She was smiling at me and being her usual happy-go-lucky self, and I realized that it was kind of ludicrous for me to be so upset with her.

"He's cute," I said with a sigh as I grabbed her purse.

"He's not *cute*," she said. "You don't call a six-foot-three guy 'cute', Ivy. He's got facial hair and muscles. He's a man."

"Handsome, then," I whispered. "He's handsome, hot, fine, whatever you want to call it. He looks good. There, I said it."

Luke Wright had a girlfriend, and I was ashamed of Britney for even thinking of him like that, and even more for making me agree with her. I smiled, though, because I knew it was out of character of me to be uptight.

"Come on," I said, putting my arm through hers. "Derek's waiting."

Chapter 6

It was past midnight when I got home.

Derek had a couple of his friends over, and they ended up staying while we watched a movie. He didn't feel like getting out to take me home, and he begged me to stay the night at his house. I could have chosen to do so, but I told him I wanted to go home.

My parents wouldn't have even asked where I was if I had decided to stay. I had been living on my own for the last two years, so they had grown accustomed to not asking where I had been or when I was coming or going. I just couldn't let myself stay the night with him. I knew what that would lead to.

Derek dropped me off in the driveway.

He kissed me, but he was a little irritated about having to get out in the cold to give me a ride home. I couldn't really blame him. It was late, and he was tired. He had to get up early to train the next day. I knew it would have been much easier for me to crash at his place. I thanked him again for the ride and told him I'd talk to him tomorrow.

The house was quiet when I went inside.

I assumed everyone was sleeping, and I went straight to my room. I wasn't trying to spy on Luke or anything, but I did glance into his bedroom. The room where he was staying was right across the hall from mine, and I couldn't help but notice that his door was slightly open. The lamp was on, so I could clearly see that the room was empty.

"Hello?" I called quietly.

The bed was still made with throw pillows lined up in a neat row. It was apparent that he had never even gotten into it. I peered around the corner and glanced at the right side of the room, thinking that maybe he was sitting at Wes's old desk.

No one.

"Hello?" I repeated. "Luke?"

Nothing.

I decided not to worry about it. Maybe he was in his parents' room, or maybe he had gone out. It wasn't really any of my business.

I took a hot bath and bundled up in my flannel pajamas. I had a pair of slippers that were lined with fleece and kept my feet nice and toasty. I stepped into them and headed to the kitchen to get a glass of water before bed.

I glanced into Luke's room again on my way. It was so weird that he wasn't in there. I thought about the time difference in London, and all the traveling he had done that day, and I knew that he should've been really tired. It crossed my mind that Britney could've come back by the house and asked him if he wanted to go somewhere. It bothered me that he wasn't in his room sleeping, and I rolled my eyes at myself for even caring.

I was standing in the kitchen, drinking a glass of water when I figured out where Luke was.

Movement coming from the backyard caught my eye, and I walked toward the window only to find that he was out there, throwing knives at my dad's target. He had on a winter coat with a thick beanie and gloves, and I stood at the window and watched as he calmly and casually threw knives at the target in a no-spin, overhand technique. He tossed slowly and softly, gently lobbing them through the air. He was standing at the ten-foot line, and all of the knives he tossed hit their mark, falling within the center target.

Once he had used the whole set, he walked over to the target and began pulling out the knives one by one. I silently jogged to the hall closet where I retrieved some cold weather gear. I put on a jacket, hat, gloves and scarf, not even caring if any of it matched.

Luke looked at me when I opened the back door. He smiled. "I hope I didn't wake you up," he said.

I shook my head. "I just got home," I said. "I didn't even hear you."

"I just got back, too," he said. "Your parents left the back door open for me, and the security lights came on when I was coming in. I saw the target, and I couldn't resist."

"Where'd you get the knives?" I asked, thinking maybe they were his and he had traveled with them.

"The mud room," he said. "Your dad showed them to me earlier. We threw a little bit. He said I could use them anytime."

"Where'd you go?" I asked.

"When?"

"You said you just got back," I said.

"Oh, I went with Jo and your brother. We went by your other brother's house and then over to Wes and Jo's place."

"Daniel?" I asked.

"Owen."

"Daniel came by, too, though. He brought Kip over to see Wes and Jo. They only stayed a little while since it was almost Kip's bedtime. Courtney wasn't feeling well."

I nodded. "She thought she'd get better after the first trimester, but this one's rough on her."

"That's what Daniel said," Luke agreed. "He said they think it's a girl this time because she feels so different."

"I thought you weren't gonna get to meet everybody till tomorrow night," I said, feeling like I had missed out on something.

He shrugged. "It was kind of a spur of the moment thing for us to go over there," he said. "I think they just couldn't wait to see Wes. Your little nephews are really cute," he added. He touched his cheek. "I think I still have baby food on my face from where one of them kissed me."

He stood at the line and faced the target, letting one of the knives fly through the air. His form and release was so delicate and gentle that I actually leaned forward a few inches as I watched it fly, trying to help the knife make it through the air and into the target.

"You're so gentle," I said.

"Gentle?" he asked, glancing at me.

"The way you throw," I clarified. "It's just so slow and soft."

"I'm just trying not to wake anybody up," he said.

"You won't," I said. "The bedrooms are on the other side of the house."

Luke let another knife go. Again, in that same slow, delicate manner.

"Can you not do it?" I asked.

"Do what?"

"Throw it harder."

He shot me an amused smile. "Yes, I can throw it harder."

"Do it," I said.

He nonchalantly turned toward the target, and without another word, he began to release the knives—all eight of them. Thwap, thwap, thwap, thwap... they flew through the air, one after another with speed and precision. He reared back and then followed through with the same overhand technique he had been using before, only this time, the motion was more intense. His movements were sharp and defined, but he still seemed somehow relaxed. I watched him, thinking I wished I could throw like that. They whizzed through the air and solidly found their home in the target. Thwap, thwap, thwap,

thwap. He finished the last of the set and turned to smile at me.

"Is that what you mean?" he asked.

I nodded wide-eyed, feeling speechless.

"You're gonna freeze out here," he said, noticing the way I was standing in a bundled-up position.

"You're gonna freeze too."

He shook his head. "I'm not cold."

"I'm not either," I said.

He grinned at me and lifted his eyebrows sardonically. I was obviously cold. I was standing like a person who was cold. My shoulders were lifted up several inches, almost touching my ears, and my hands were clasped in front of my face.

"Are you coming in?" I asked.

"I wasn't, but I can," he said.

"Okay." I nodded and headed into the house, knowing he'd follow me.

"I thought you'd be exhausted by now," I said once he retrieved the knives from the target and made his way into the house. We stood by the door, and both of us worked on taking off our winter gear. I reached out, locking the deadbolt.

"I should probably try to go to bed," he said. "I just didn't feel tired when they dropped me off. I slept some on the plane."

I set my coat, hat, and gloves on a nearby chair. Luke set my dad's knives on the catchall before shrugging out of his coat. He took his shoes off and left them by the door before pulling off his beanie.

He had a short-ish haircut, and his thick, dark hair didn't seem to be affected at all by the removal of the hat. He ran his hand through it and gave it a shake just in case.

"How about you?" he asked. "Aren't you tired? I thought you had school tomorrow."

"I do, but my first class isn't until eleven."

He nodded, glancing toward the hallway as if assuming that we were going to head that direction.

"You wanna hang out for a few minutes before we hit the sack?" I asked.

"Sure," he said. He followed me to the couch.

I sat cross-legged in the corner and he chose a spot next to me, leaving a few feet of space between us. He still had on that same Bishop Motorcycles sweatshirt, and I smiled absentmindedly, thinking I wanted one like it.

Seeing it reminded me of something... "What's up with your dad not wanting you to work at the dealership?"

Luke let out a little humorless laugh, shaking his head. "You noticed that, huh?"

I nodded, but otherwise stayed silent, waiting for him to continue.

He lifted one shoulder, seeming maybe a little reluctant to explain. "My, uh, biological parents. They were... uh... not... really... I don't know. They weren't really great people, I guess."

I felt a little heartbroken by his tone and sincerity, and I wanted to tell him that he didn't have to continue. I really didn't know what this had to do with his dad not liking motorcycles.

"You don't need to tell me if—"

"No, it's okay, I'm just trying to figure out how to say it. It's something I've thought of, but no one's ever really asked me, so I've never said it out loud. Plus, I don't want to come across as offensive since your family works with motorcycles and everything. It's not that my dad has anything against them, it's just that..." He took a breath, searching for the right words. "My birth parents were kind of... I don't know how to say this other than... trashy," he said. "They didn't choose to give me up for adoption, I was taken from them. There were definitely drugs involved. Meth, I think, and other things. They had both bccn in-and-out of jail for different things. Anyway, there was a big incident right after I was born—a bust or whatever, and the state just took me away from them and found a better home for me."

My heart pounded as he spoke. His raw honesty was touching, and I imagined him as a helpless little baby being born into those less-than-ideal circumstances. I had to resist the urge to reach out and touch his arm—to try to comfort him, or at least let him know I didn't judge him.

"Have you ever seen or talked to them?" I asked.

He nodded, glancing at the hallway to make sure no one was listening to us. "Not in person, but I've seen pictures. I know my real mom's name, so I looked her up on Facebook like five or six years ago.

Longer than that, actually. It was back before we moved to London."

"What'd you find?"

He shrugged. "Everything I dreaded. A life I'm glad I escaped. It's just a completely different circumstance than the one I'm in with the Wrights. She's got other kids. I think I might have two brothers. That was pretty crazy, seeing a picture of them—especially since they kinda look like me."

"Did you talk to her?"

He shook his head. "I just looked at her profile for a few minutes. I pretty much regretted doing it. My parents didn't even know I searched her out. They still don't know. It kind of freaked me out, honestly. I was so relieved and happy that my life had turned out differently than what I saw in those pictures. I just turned off the computer and vowed never to look at Facebook again." He gave me a little smile. "If there is some good that came from it, it's that I can understand what my dad's so afraid of. It makes me a lot more patient with him."

Chapter 7

"What do you mean by that?" I asked, staring at the side of Luke's face. "Why do you have to be patient with him?"

He sighed. "I don't want to offend you because your family's so deep into motorcycles and everything, but I think... I guess just part of me thinks that's why my dad's so weird about my work... why he wants me to pick something else to do."

"Why? Because he thinks motorcycles are trashy?"

Luke glanced at me with a self-deprecating smile, shaking his head a little like he wasn't getting things across in the right way. "See? That's what I was afraid of. I don't want you to think that he—"

"I don't think anything," I said. "I'm just trying to figure out what you're saying. Do you think your dad doesn't want you to work at the shop because he's afraid you'll turn out like your birthparents?"

"When you put it like that, it makes it seem like he's really rude or judgmental, and it's not like that. He's a good person. And I don't even really know if that's what he thinks. I'm just saying... he and my mom pretty much rescued me from that situation. It makes sense to me that he wouldn't want me to go back to that kind of life... that he would want to do anything he could to prevent me from turning out like them. Don't get me wrong. Obviously, I know there's nothing wrong with motorcycles, otherwise I wouldn't be so passionate about them. They've just got a certain... air of rebellion, I guess, that surrounds them, and in the back of my mind, I feel like maybe that's why Dad's so reluctant to see me take that path. I mean, he's gotten better now that Jo's with Wes and he knows about your family business and sees that you're so successful. But he would still really like to see me go to college and probably choose a different career."

I stared at the side of his face. His profile was so different from Derek's. He was just different than Derek in general. I could see things in him that weren't just physical—I could see character. He was honest and vulnerable yet, at the same time, resolute and unyielding.

I experienced a lot of conflicting emotions in that moment. At the surface, I felt guilty for ever bringing up the fact that Luke looked different from his family. I was really embarrassed that I had pointed it out earlier, especially now that I knew there were deeper emotions tied to the subject.

But something deeper inside me admired him. I remembered the way he had handled his dad earlier—the way he patiently deflected his dad's comments without seeming irritated or defensive.

"I think it's amazing that you're following your dream," I said. "That takes courage."

He smiled without looking at me. "Thank you," he said. "I've thought about just going to college and doing something else, just to please him, reassure him, but that just doesn't seem right. It's not me. I could probably choose to do something fairly close, you know, some kind of mechanical engineering or something, but I wouldn't be happy settling for doing something I don't love, and then I'd ultimately be mad at him about it."

"I think it's amazing that you know that," I said.

He shrugged. "I don't know if it's amazing, but it's just where I'm at. It doesn't seem like an option for me to give up on something I love. You're surrounded by people who do that, though. Your boyfriend, your parents, grandparents, siblings… you guys are all dream-chasers."

I sighed, feeling like that was just about the sweetest compliment ever. "Do you think your dad will eventually stop giving you a hard time about it?"

"I honestly don't feel like what he does now is giving me a hard time. He's much better than he used to be."

"So, what do you want to do? Work at the dealership?"

"I'm gonna be a designer," he said. "Not that I want to ever stop working in the repair shop, because I don't. I truly do love taking a machine that's broken and making it run again. It makes me happy to do that. But I do want to design and build some new machines. I'm gonna start by winning that contest your dad was talking about."

"Don't you have to come here for that?" I asked. "You know, work at the headquarters?"

Luke shook his head. "Everything's digital nowadays. I could design anywhere."

"Your sister would love it if you moved here, though," I said. "But I guess your parents wouldn't, or your girlfriend."

"Speaking of girlfriend," he said. "What are you gonna do next month when Derek leaves?"

I shrugged. "Miss him, I guess."

"I thought maybe you'd travel with him."

"I'm here till May, at least. That's when I graduate. I guess I thought I'd just figure it out after that. He'll be in Cleveland by then. He talks like he wants me to move up there with him, but that'll mean moving into his house, and I'm not sure. Even if I was ready to move in with him, there are other things to consider. The players don't take their significant others on every trip. I'd be staying in Cleveland quite a bit by myself, which would be weird since I don't know anyone there."

"I bet the other wives and girlfriends are in the same boat. I'm sure you can get to know some of them."

"That's what Derek said." I shrugged. "I don't know. It's weird to think about moving in with him. It's weird thinking about having him gone for so long, too. Both things are weird. Both options seem bad. I'm just kind of putting off thinking about it."

Luke took in a long, deep breath, one that signaled that he was about to wrap up the conversation. He scooted to the edge of the couch stretching by lifting his arms upward. "I better get some sleep," he said.

"I better, too," I agreed.

He stood up and extended a hand, offering to help me up. I took his assistance even though I was perfectly capable of standing on my own. He clasped his big hand around mine and pulled me to my feet. He was smiling at me as he did it, and I returned his smile, feeling like I was cheating on Derek just for letting Luke help me up off the couch. Maybe it was because his hand wrapped around mine gave me a tingling sensation in my stomach. I broke contact with him as soon as the thought crossed my mind. I would no longer be able to touch this guy. No more physical contact. Something was wrong if he could cause me to have butterflies just from helping me stand up.

"Thanks," I said stiffly. "For the talk," I added out of sheer nerves.

He smiled. "Thank you," he said. "I hope you don't think negatively about my dad. He's really a good—"

"I like your dad," I said. "I can completely understand why he would be wary. I mean not that he should be, but I can see what you mean. I think he's just trying to protect you or whatever."

Luke nodded. "Night," he said.

"Night."

I expected him to walk with me down the hall, but instead, he headed toward the back door.

"Where are you going?" I asked.

"To get my coat and shoes, and put your dad's knives away."

"You can just leave the knives there," I said. "We can put them up in the morning."

"I hate to do that," he said. He hesitated, staring at me with a look of concern. "Wait, are you scared? Did you need me to walk you to your room or something?"

I smiled. He genuinely thought I might be scared to cross the house by myself. "Yes," I said, nodding and wearing a reluctant expression, even though I was not scared at all and had lived in a house by myself for the last two years. He was just so sweet that I couldn't resist playing with him.

"Well, walk with me to put your dad's knives up," he said. "I'm not leaving them out. He's gonna know it was me who used them."

"I'm just messing with you," I said. "I'm not scared. Go ahead and put Dad's knives up. I'm going to bed. I'll see you tomorrow."

He nodded. "Sounds good."

He had already taken a step or two away from me, so there was a little gap between us. I knew we were taking off in different directions. I had already decided not to touch him again, but in those brief seconds of awkward hesitation, I did the unthinkable. I lunged toward him, and gave him a hug. I have no idea why I did it. It was almost involuntary. I blame the fact that I had been raised in a hugging family.

"Night," I repeated, patting him on the back.

Luke was stiff at first when he caught me in his arms, but he quickly relaxed and squeezed me back. "Night, Ivy," he said.

In those split seconds, my face was right up against his chest. He smelled masculine and clean. This combined with the familiar logo on his sweatshirt gave me more of those undesired sensations. Plus, I could feel his muscular build. I let go of him quickly, stepping back.

"I'm sorry. We're just huggers. My whole family. My mom probably already hugged you a bunch. We all do it. You're gonna get lots of them while you're here."

"I hear they're good for you," he said smiling at me from over his shoulder as he walked toward the door to retrieve my dad's knives.

"Yep, that's what I hear, too," I said casually.

Dork, dork, triple dork. What in the world? We're all huggers? What was wrong with me? This was not at all what was supposed to be happening.

I went straight to my room, closed the door, and sat on my bed.

I had a sinking, guilty feeling in the pit of my stomach. I almost felt as if I was woozy or seasick. Until Derek, I hadn't really found a guy who gave me the desire to make a commitment. And now, here I was, only a few months into this committed relationship, and I felt undeniably drawn to another man.

God, help my wandering thoughts.

God, help my wandering eyes.

Give me the strength to ignore Luke.

Blind me to his looks.

Help me to be unattracted to him.

Then, as they often do, my own thoughts interrupted my prayers. I started thinking things like: You're not married, Ivy. There's no need to ask for forgiveness or feel guilty for looking at Luke.

The thought of looking at Luke sent an image across my mind. I recalled the sight of him throwing those knives into the target—the way he quickly and expertly sent them sailing through the air one after another.

I squeezed my eyes shut tight, begging myself to stop imagining him. I was committed to Derek, and it was just plain unacceptable for me to entertain thoughts of another man.

God, help me to know what's right.

Give me strength to honor my commitments.

Then, I thought of something that would give me strength—the sight of Derek. I grabbed my phone and began typing his name into the search engine.

I only had to type his first name, and there he was—Derek Holbrook—number one on the list of Dereks, followed by Derek Carr and Derek Jeter. I clicked on his name, and his Wikipedia page came up, along with several photos—all baseball mugshots with Derek wearing his Indians cap. I read the words on the entry.

Derek Holbrook
Baseball second baseman
Derek Alexander Holbrook is an American professional baseball second baseman for the Cleveland Indians of Major League Baseball.
Spouse: Unmarried
Salary: 14 million (USD)

I sighed, and clicked on the icon at the top of the screen that said "images". The photos that came up were more than just mug shots in his baseball cap. There were so many pictures of him. Some of him swinging a bat, some of him making plays in the field, some laughing and high-fiving his teammates.

I smiled and took a deep breath as I looked at them, thanking God that I had this resource to go to. I reminded myself how very fortunate I was to be the girlfriend of this man. I reminded myself that I had a crush on him for years, and that I would be a fool to look at anyone else.

I don't know what I was thinking getting butterflies with Luke. I wasn't thinking. It was just something that happened. It was uncontrollable.

There was only one thing to do. I had to abstain from physical contact with him. No more letting him help me up off the couch, and definitely no more hugging. I would do the right thing and control my wandering eyes, that's all there was to it.

I went to bed that night, feeling thoroughly repentant and free of any guilt.

Tomorrow was a new day—one where I would think of Luke Wright as nothing more than a friend, nothing more than Jolene's brother.

Chapter 8

Luke

Luke Wright could, one hundred percent, understand why his sister had married Wes Bishop and picked up her life to move to Memphis with his family.

He would have done the same thing if their roles were reversed. After only five days of staying at Jesse and Rose Bishop's house, he realized just how special their family was.

He had heard the phrase "family first" before, but the Bishops gave new meaning to it. They were the epitome of a strong, supportive family. They had each other's backs no matter what. In the last five days, he had been in awe of the way they interacted with each other. They played games, threw knives, rode motorcycles, sang songs, talked, ate meals, laughed, and just flat out enjoyed each other's presence.

They were in no hurry to run off and obtain other things because they already had everything they needed. It was like they had something simple but profound figured out—like you could just choose to be happy and content, and therefore you *were* happy and content.

That's not to say that they didn't have trials, because they did. Luke heard them talking about some drama with Darcy's parents who were now deceased. Apparently, her late father had been into real estate and that's how she and Owen owned the house where Wes and Jolene were living. They didn't go into anything in detail, but Luke gathered that there had been some bad blood with Owen and Darcy's late father.

Even when the less-than-perfect subject was brought up, they were all still so positive and upbeat. Luke's parents were like this in many ways, but the Bishops took it to another level. Maybe it was because there were so many of them that it seemed especially impressive. It just felt good to hang around so many positive people. If there had been an eligible Bishop for Luke to marry, he would have done it himself, complete with the move to Memphis and everything.

Who was he kidding? It wasn't just any Bishop he wished was eligible. It was Ivy. Beautiful, sweet Ivy. He loved everything about her. He loved watching her get in trouble by saying exactly what was on her mind. He loved watching her blush, and laugh, and cut up with her brothers and their wives and children. If things were different, Luke would have had it bad for Ivy. If they were both single, he would have looked at Ivy in a totally different way.

They had spent a lot of time together in the last five days—had gotten to know each other as friends.

From what she said, she usually spent most of her free time with Derek, but this week had been different. Wes was just moving home, and there was company in the house, which meant there were a few big, family dinners. Derek came to most of them, but instead of leaving and going to his house or going out afterward like they normally did, Derek left by himself, and Ivy stayed and hung out with family.

Luke was happy she made that choice because she was a bright light—like a ray of sunshine. She never met a stranger. She had tons of friends, many of whom she spoke about, and a few whom Luke had met during his stay.

Luke was thinking about Ivy because he wanted to see her. He and his parents would be heading to the airport within the hour, and he hated to leave without telling her goodbye.

He was a little concerned because the evening before, Ivy had mentioned wanting to go for a ride after dinner, but instead, she left the house without a word to anybody. He had seen her drive away, and he remembered the look on her face. She didn't look happy. He heard her parents speculating on her whereabouts, but it was really none of his business, so he tried not to seem too interested.

He went to bed at midnight, and Ivy still wasn't home. She was home that morning when he woke up. He saw her car in the driveway and noticed that her bedroom door was closed, but he hadn't seen her at all.

They had just finished eating lunch and were still all in the kitchen area when his mom asked Rose about Ivy. He listened to their conversation.

"I hope we get to tell sweet Ivy 'goodbye' before we go," Ginger said.

"I'm sure you will," Rose said. "She's not feeling her best this morning, but I'm sure she'll come out to see you guys off."

"Oh, I'm sorry to hear that," Ginger said. "She doesn't have to come out. Just tell her how much we enjoyed getting to know her this week."

"I will," Rose said. "But I'll go in there in a little bit and see if she feels up to coming out here to tell y'all goodbye."

The women moved on to other subjects like Wes and Jolene and the fact that Ginger was so happy and thankful that her daughter was being so well taken care of.

It was difficult for Luke to concentrate on anything but the fact that Ivy was ill. He wondered what had made her sick and thought about the flu or food poisoning. Surely there was something he could do to bring her some comfort. He headed toward the hall, trying to talk himself out of knocking on her door.

Jesse Bishop was coming out of Ivy's room as Luke entered the hallway. Their eyes met and Luke gave the man a casual nod as if he had been planning on going to his own room. Jesse smiled and nodded back, but his smile was forced and laced with worry or disappointment.

This caused Luke to worry instantly. He almost said, "Is she okay?" his mouth was open and he was poised to let the words come out, but then he noticed that Jesse had left the door of her room cracked open. Luke made the split-second decision that rather than ask, he would just see for himself.

He stepped into the bedroom across the hall while Jesse disappeared, but once the coast was clear, he made his way into the hall again. He used a knuckle and tapped on Ivy's door a few times.

Nothing.

He thought her heard her voice, and he put his ear to the crack in the door.

"Ivy?" he said with his ear to the door.

He heard her voice responding, but he couldn't tell what she had said.

"Ivy?" He pushed the door a little more, and peered inside, expecting to see her sprawled out on her bed.

Her bed was empty. It was a mess, like she had been in it and had just gotten out, but it was empty nonetheless.

"Ivy?" he said, peeking into her room.

"Hello?" she said.

"Hey, where are you?" he asked quietly, stepping into her room.

There was some kind of noise happening—maybe a fan or some kind of white noise machine that just sounded like a fan.

"Because I didn't feel like talking, that's why." she said in a frustrated tone.

Her voice was high pitched like a whimper, and the words she said didn't make any sense to him. She took in several gasping breaths—hitching breaths, as if she was crying.

"No, Kade, you can't come over," she said.

Luke had already come into her room, but he stopped in his tracks when he realized she wasn't talking to him. He took a step back in an effort to quietly retreat, but he saw movement on the other side of her bed, and he froze. He saw her hand come up and then go down again like she was running it through her hair. She was sitting on the floor, facing the other direction. The shades were drawn, making it dark in there for mid-day—certainly darker than the rest of the house. The only light coming in was through the cracks in the blinds.

"You can't come over. We've still got people over here. And I don't feel like talking, anyway. I just picked up because I wanted to talk to you before... before Britney did."

Again, she took in a deep, shuttering breath making it obvious that she was crying.

"I can't even say her name, Kade. I can't believe what she did. She's been my best friend since... hang on..."

She trailed off, letting out a long, wheezing cry followed by several gasps. Her voice was weak and vulnerable. Luke knew he should walk out. He knew he should leave, but he was paralyzed, stunned, he felt like his feet were stuck to the floor. He had to know what Britney had done—what it was that was making Ivy so upset. He felt red-hot anger at the sound of her pitiful voice.

"*She* did!" Ivy said. "She told me. That's how I know. She called me yesterday and said she couldn't live with the guilt." (gasp, gasp, gasp) "She said it just *happened*. She said they were drinking and that it just happened without her really even knowing what was going on, can you believe that? I told her that doesn't *just happen*. You have to *let* it happen. You have to *want* it to happen."

She paused, and Luke knew the person on the other end was speaking.

"She cried and apologized," Ivy said. "She said she'd never intentionally do anything to hurt me and begged me to forgive her. She bawled her eyes out like she expected me to feel bad for her. "

Another long pause.

"Two nights ago. After we had dinner at Shug's. Derek was having some friends over afterward, and I guess… she… went… over… there."

She gasped again, several times.

Luke closed his eyes and clinched his fists, feeling like he wanted to hurt someone—specifically Derek Holbrook.

"No, I haven't told my dad. He would want to hurt him. He just came in here, and I told them I was sick."

There was more gasping, followed by a deep, calming breath as if she was trying to make herself quit crying.

"Yeah, I went over there last night," she said. "He begged me to forgive him. He said everyone was drinking and Britney just threw herself at him. He said she said things like... hang on... I really can't believe I'm about to repeat this. He said she kept saying that all these years, she's had to s-sit back and watch while I... got...everything. She said it was her... t-turn... now."

She let out another long, wheezing sob followed by a long pause.

"No," she said, finally. "If we were sleeping together, it never would have happened. Derek said that's why he was weak when she threw herself at him."

(A pause.)

"He begged me to forgive him."

(Another pause.)

"I want to. I mean, from what he said, Britney basically forced him to do it."

(Pause.)

"I know it takes two, Kade, but he swore it would never happen again. He promised on his career."

(Pause.)

"No," she said bluntly. "I never want to see or talk to her again. I almost want to get a new phone number. She's blowing up my text. I haven't talked to her since I talked to Derek. She doesn't know I know all that about her saying she had to watch... me... whatever. I'm not talking to her. I'm not friends with her anymore."

(Pause.)

"I don't know," Ivy said. "I haven't decided about Derek. Part of me wants to forgive him because I know it's all her fault. When I left his house last night, I told him I needed time to think. He's begging to come over here, but I can't handle that drama right now. We've still got people at our house, and my parents are here. I'm gonna have to wait until I can get myself together enough to go over there. I can't think straight right now."

(Pause.)

"I don't really care. That's on you if you want to be friends with her, but I'm done. I've been up all night, and I feel like crap. I can't even believe she told me it happened. Part of me wishes she would've just kept it from me. I feel like she just *wanted* me to find out so we'd break up."

Ivy took another unsteady breath, but this time, she shifted. Luke could see the top of her head move, and he assumed she was about to get up.

He took two silent steps, making his way out of her room and into the hallway, leaving the door open so she wouldn't notice the movement.

He absolutely hated knowing Ivy was in pain. He felt like he had to do something.

Chapter 9

I had been up all night, crying.

Betrayal was a bitter pill to swallow, and all night, I had tossed and turned in my bed, wrestling with anger and embarrassment. I imagined them together—my boyfriend and my best friend doing things that even he and I hadn't done. I had spent so many hours with him during the last few months, and now Britney knew him intimately. It was the worst thing I could possibly imagine her doing, and she did it.

What made it even harder was that she threw herself at him. It wasn't like he tricked her into doing it. The opposite was true. Derek said she basically gave him no choice. He said he didn't even enjoy it—hated himself over it.

All night, I replayed my conversation with Britney—the one where she came to me in tears *needing to tell me the truth.* I thought of the conversation that followed—the one I had with Derek—the one where he told me the whole story, the way it really happened. He begged me to forgive him, told me he loved me, and swore on his life it would never happen again.

All night, I replayed those conversations and then I imagined the two of them together. Anger and jealousy had stolen my sleep, and now I found myself delirious, heartbroken, lovesick, and pretty much sick in general.

I honestly didn't know how to go on with my life. I felt like I had been broken into a thousand pieces and it was simply impossible for me to get put back together the same way I was before—like I would somehow forever be changed by this.

I was utterly devastated at the thought of losing my best friend and a boyfriend in one fell swoop. I was so mad at Britney that I almost wanted to forgive Derek just so she had no chance of being with him.

My feelings were all over the map.

Constant texts bombarded my phone from both of them, begging me for forgiveness. I really didn't want to talk about it, but all the pent-up emotions were just eating away at me, so I broke down the following day and told Kade. He said that I should take a day or two to think about it before I went running back to Derek.

I really didn't want his advice. I only called him so that he would take my side in cutting ties with Britney. He said she was a terrible person for doing something like that, but unfortunately, his statement didn't make me feel any better. I hung up the phone with him, feeling guilty and embarrassed for having told him in the first place.

Horrible.

Terrible.

Ridiculously bad.

That's how I felt.

I wanted to crawl under a rock and never come out. My mom came into my room to try to get me to go out and tell the Wrights goodbye, but I knew my face was red and my eyes were swollen, so I told her I was just too sick to get out of bed.

I stayed on the edge of my bed, staring at the wall and feeling broken. I hadn't even noticed that my mom had left my bedroom door open until someone knocked on it. I turned and glanced in that direction, noticing that someone was there.

It was Luke. He was standing in the doorway, but he was staring downward where all I could see was his profile. He was giving me privacy until I invited him in.

It broke my heart to see him waiting there.

I had enjoyed getting to know him, and I wanted to be able to give him a sincere farewell, but I was simply incapable of doing that. I was currently out of commission as a human being.

I grabbed the pillow that was next to me, and covered my face with it. "Come in," I said, in a muffled tone.

I heard him crossing the room, and the next thing I knew, he was sitting on the very edge of the bed, right next to me. I couldn't see his face, but I saw his body through a crack under the pillow.

"Are you okay?" he asked.

"Yeah," I said, trying my best to sound 'okay'.

"Why do you have your face covered?"

"Because I have a bad headache."

There was a long pause, followed by a sigh. "We're leaving," he said.

"I know. I'm sorry. I'm sick. I had a lot of fun with you this week. I'm glad you came."

"I had fun too," he said.

He sighed again, and I felt his hand touch my arm. I glanced down at it, feeling tears sting my eyes at the embarrassment of having to sit there with my face covered. I seriously hated Britney for bringing me to this.

"You're gonna be okay, Ivy," Luke said. "This, too, soon shall pass."

"I know. I'm just sick."

"Okay, well they're waiting on me out there, so..." he trailed off, hesitating.

"Okay," I said. "I'm glad you came. Tell your parents it was really nice meeting them."

Luke didn't respond to my statement. He just picked up my hand and gave it a squeeze. I didn't know what he was doing at first. I felt him grab my hand and bring it upward and then I felt a warm squeeze—like he was hugging me with just our hands. My gut clinched at the feel of it. He only meant it to comfort me, but I was already on edge, and the physical contact caused a wave of emotion to hit me. Just as soon as he squeezed me, however, he set my arm down, resting it in the same position it was in before.

"Can I see your face before I go?" he asked quietly.

I lifted the pillow that was covering my face. I wanted to look at him, but I couldn't bring myself to do it. I kept my eyes closed, knowing he was staring down at me. I felt his hand touch the side of my face, and I just stayed there, completely still. His fingertip (or his thumb, I couldn't tell) lightly touched my tearstained cheek.

"Bye, Ivy," he said softly.

"Bye," I said.

I wanted so badly to look at him, but my eyes were glued shut. I heard him take a breath, and then I felt him stand up. He walked around my bed and then out of my room.

I cried.

I was so mad at myself for being incapable of seeing Luke and his family off. I really did have a lot of fun getting to know them, and it only added to my shame that I was physically unable to get out of my bed and give them a proper sendoff.

***

Two days passed.

I didn't come out of my bedroom for two whole days.

I hadn't told my family what happened.

I wasn't going to be friends with Britney anymore, but I hadn't yet decided what I would do about Derek, so I refrained from telling them any of the details. If I told them what happened, they would

90

not approve of me staying with Derek, so I decided to wait until I was certain. I didn't want the added pressure. I wanted to make the decision on my own.

I didn't talk to anyone during those days, not Derek, or Kade, or any of my other friends. I sent Derek a text to let him know my family didn't know anything because I didn't want him to call or come by. I told him I'd be in touch after I took a couple of days to cool down, and he messaged me back saying he loved me and that I could take all the time I needed. He said he would be waiting for me.

I stayed in my room and did some much-needed book binging and soul searching. I didn't even go to school. My parents thought I had a stomach bug, which was sort of the truth since I wasn't eating and my digestive system was a complete mess.

Finally, after two days, I took a shower, got dressed, and decided to face the light of day.

My eyes and cheeks were still sore and tight from crying. I felt a bit like a vampire or someone who was allergic to the sun, but I had to put one foot in front of the other and step out of my room, otherwise I might just stay in there for the rest of my life.

It was Friday, and I only had one class, so I decided to go to it. I thought I might go to Derek's that night and talk to him for a while. I wanted to be with him, but I didn't know if I could. I honestly didn't know if I could get over what he had done.

It was such a sad situation for me. I had wanted him for so long, considered him the man of my dreams. And then, when I finally got him, this happened. I felt like our relationship had been tainted, and by my best friend, of all people.

I had no idea what I was going to do.

I thought maybe seeing Derek and talking to him in person would help me decide. My mom had come into my room earlier that morning before she and Dad went to the shop. She was happy to hear that I was feeling up to going to school and said she was relieved that neither she nor Dad had 'caught the bug'.

They were both gone by the time I left for class.

It was a chilly morning. I had been so numb and out-of-it for the last few days that the sudden change in temperature was a welcome shock to my system.

My car was parked in the garage, but my mom (as she often did) left the big door open. Our garage was facing the back of the property, and both of my parents had a habit of not closing the doors. That meant it was now freezing in there.

I planned on starting my car and going back into the house while I gave it a few minutes to warm up, but I got sidetracked. There was a folded piece of paper in the driver's seat. I reached out to move it before I sat down and started the car. I was cold, but I was too curious not to open it right then. I made sure the door was closed tightly and turned on my heater before carefully unfolding the piece of notebook paper.

I don't know what I expected.

I think I expected it to be a note from Derek or from Britney.

It was indeed a note, but I instantly scanned to the bottom of the page, only to find that there was no signature. I had no idea who had written it. I didn't recognize the hand writing, either. It was almost as if the person who wrote it had taken care for me *not* to be able to recognize it. It was written in perfect block print—all caps—the neatest, straightest handwriting I had ever seen.

Feeling a little confused and a lot curious, I started at the beginning and began to read.

Sweet Ivy,

I'm sorry you're hurting. I wish there was something I could do to reverse your situation, or at least take away your pain. While it might not be any of my business, I couldn't resist offering my thoughts about what happened with Derek and Britney. Ultimately, it's your choice if you want to forgive him. I am a believer in forgiveness and restoration. I am not perfect, and God knows, I need forgiveness and mercy on a continual basis.

That being said, you were not wrong for making him wait. On the contrary, he was wrong for telling you that his disloyalty had anything to do with you. It had nothing to do with you. Please do not blame yourself for his weakness. You deserve better. When you're in a committed relationship, you deserve to know, beyond the shadow of a doubt, that there would never ever be a betrayal like the one you've just had to deal with. I'm not saying Derek can't become a man who is worthy of your trust. Maybe this will be the wakeup call he needed. Perhaps forgiveness is the route to take. That's between you, Derek, and God.

But please know that there are men in the world who are loyal and trustworthy. There are men who would love you the way you deserve to be loved. There are men who would never, ever be unfaithful to you.

You, Ivy, are a prize, a treasure, a precious jewel. You truly deserve unwavering loyalty, commitment, and love. Please don't settle for anything less than that.

Instead of a signature, there was a reference to scripture at the bottom of the page.

Philippians 4:8

My heart was racing as I scanned the letter, marveling at the words and the penmanship.

It obviously wasn't Derek or Britney who had written it. The only person it could be was Kade. It was a little too articulate and confident for Kade, but he was the only one who could have written it.

I read it again slowly before searching the Bible verse. It was a list of things we should think of. It said we should think of things that are noble, right, pure, lovely, admirable, excellent, and praiseworthy.

I smiled as I read the list, thinking they were pretty much the opposite of the things I'd been dwelling on for the last few days.

I drove to class.

I parked, walked across campus, and went through all the motions of going to school. I had talked myself into believing this was my fault—that it wouldn't have ever happened if I had made sure Derek's needs were met.

But this letter changed everything for me.

Not only did it give me confidence to know that I was worthy of loyalty, but it also literally gave me a list of things to think about. Anytime my mind started to wander back to my pain and drama, I thought of that list.

Noble. I thought of things like royalty. Kings and queens, and knights in shining armor.

Right. As a math girl, I thought of right angles— a perfect ninety degrees.

Pure. Snow, twenty-four carat gold, water, the ocean. My mind went to the ocean for some reason when I thought of the word pure.

Lovely. There was one I really liked. The word lovely just resonated with me. I loved to imagine lovely things. I thought of things like rope swings and motorcycle rides on long, windy roads. I thought of spring days and fresh flowers, and blueberry pancakes with butter and syrup. I thought of giving dogs belly rubs and drinking a tall glass of water when you're really thirsty.

Admirable. I knew if something was *admire-able*, that meant it was worthy of being admired. That was a great word in itself, and I would probably think on it at a later time, but for now, it made me think of *admiral*. This was a completely different word, but I still liked it. It brought to mind an orange and black butterfly. I figured that was just as pleasant as admirable, so I went with it.

Excellent. There was another word I really liked—excellent. I just liked the way it sounded and the way it looked when it was written. It also brought specific things to mind, like A's on tests and gold medals.

And lastly, there was praiseworthy—things that were worthy of praise. This obviously brought God to mind. And who wouldn't be comforted by that?

I thought of that letter and its contents all during class. It was exactly what I needed, and my heart swelled with thankfulness toward Kade for taking the time to write it for me and leave it in my car.

Honestly, it kind of made me feel differently about him—like something existed in his personality that I didn't know was there before. It wasn't like I went from having no feelings toward him to being in love with him, but the letter definitely changed how

I saw him. It made me view him as more of a man than I thought he was before.

Chapter 10

Over a year later.

Fourteen months, to be exact.

A lot had happened in my life since I had broken up with Derek.

I still managed to graduate that May despite the fact that my spring semester got off to a rocky start.

Derek begged me to stay with him—said it was a one-time mistake and that it would never, ever happen again.

Part of me wanted to believe him, but there was something deep inside me that knew he wasn't a hundred percent trustworthy. The funny thing was that I kind of knew it before the thing with Britney ever happened. It was a truth I hated to come to terms with because it was fun to date a famous baseball player. But I just knew in my heart that being with him was a gamble.

I was too good for gambles.

The letter Kade wrote told me that, and it was something that sank into my heart like a seed sinks into soil. Something beautiful sprouted out of that seed, something beyond words. If I had to try to put a label on it, I would call it patience and self-worth, but it was so much more than that.

I knew God would bring along someone I could fully trust. I thought, at first, that maybe Kade's letter was a sign that he was the one. It moved me so deeply that I thought for sure I was meant to develop feelings for him. I prayed for that to happen. I prayed that I would feel attraction toward him, but I just never did.

Finally, after weeks of wishing I could fall in love with Kade, I decided that some things were not to be forced. Sure, he had done something wonderful that helped pull me out of a potentially hazardous situation, but that didn't mean that we needed to fall in love. He was a good friend to me, and his letter helped me more than I could ever say, but I just never felt chemistry with him. I felt more chemistry with his letter than I did with the actual person, which was odd but true. So, Kade and I were still friends, and would always remain that way.

Britney and I weren't friends anymore, but we weren't enemies, either. After much soul searching and council from my family, I decided to forgive her. Yes, I ended up telling my family what happened. Britney had been such a fixture in our house for so many years that I knew I couldn't get away with simply saying that 'we stopped hanging out' or some other half-hearted excuse like that.

We met at a coffee shop a few months after it happened and had a long conversation. I was honest with her. I told her things changed in our relationship—that we could no longer be the kind of friends we were before it happened. We couldn't move forward and pretend it never took place, because it did. Things were different between us because of it. I did, however, forgive her. I truly forgave her, not just to her face at the coffee shop, but in my heart.

I didn't tell her that Derek told me the things she said about having to *watch me get everything all those years*. But that was in the back of my mind, and oddly enough, it made me feel bad for her, which made forgiving her easier.

The drama with Derek and Britney only took up a small piece of my life—like a glitch or hiccup. I could have let it consume me, but I chose to forgive them, put the whole thing out of my mind, and move on. Kade's letter certainly helped.

I went on to bigger and better things. I graduated, got a job, and broke ground on my new house. I had also done a little traveling.

A few of months ago, Wes went on tour to promote his new album. He started with a trip to the West Coast—Seattle, Portland, San Francisco, Los Angeles, San Diego. I was extremely busy with work, but I took a few days off and went to join him in Portland and San Francisco, which was a lot of fun.

Jolene had planned on going with him, but she wasn't feeling up to it. She thought she had mono because she kept feeling lousy, but then she found out that she was pregnant. They hadn't been trying to have a baby, so it didn't even cross her mind to check for that. She was now four months along and feeling good enough to join him on the road. They were currently in Chicago.

My job and house were things I hadn't expected, but I honestly couldn't be happier with both of them. I thought I might get my graduate degrees and get a job teaching college, but something else came across my path—something I had never considered.

Daniel and Courtney owned an art center downtown. They provided low-cost art classes and lessons for Memphis's youth. They strictly dealt with the arts—music, dance, theatre, fashion, etc. However, Courtney saw an undeniable need for academic tutoring and mentorship. She approached me about it, and long story short, I have found my calling.

I rented a house that was located in the business district not far from Courtney's art center. With the help of my family, I opened a nonprofit called Memphis Learning Center in that location. I had no idea there was such a need for this type of service. We had only been open for six months, and we were already assisting sixty-five kids in after-school programs. I had three other teachers helping me, and I'd soon need a fourth. Kade volunteered two days a week, but we really needed someone more full-time as a science instructor.

It wasn't just academic tutoring, either. It turned out to be so much more than that. We had just poured concrete for a small basketball court behind the tutoring facility. These kids truly needed role-models, people who cared, and it was an honor to think that we could somehow be a positive influence in their lives. I was still in the beginning stages of this adventure, but I could already tell I would find fulfillment through it, and for that, I was truly thankful.

So, yes, it had been an eventful year—one full of emotion, taking chances, and new beginnings. I was tired at the end of every week, but it was the good type of tired, not the kind you get from drudgery.

I was currently at the end of one of those long weeks. My neck and back were aching, and I was thankful that there would be a hot meal waiting for me at Shug and Doozy's house when I got there.

"Wuzzzup, pee-po?" I yelled, opening the door. I heard ruckus going on in the house before I could even see anyone. The kids had heard me come in, and they all ran to the door like a stampede, tackling me. Kip was three, Cora was two, and the twins would be two in a few months. They all yelled and piled on top me right there in the entryway, and I growled and tried to tickle them all at the same time.

Liam and Taylor's baby, Mack, was eleven months old and just learning to walk. He toddled behind the others, looking hilariously off-balance. Taylor followed him just to make sure he reached his destination, and Courtney came with her, carrying their newest addition on her hip, a nine-month-old princess named Eden.

"She almost jumped off of my hip trying to get over here and see what her cousins were doing," Courtney said, shaking her head.

I gave out kisses and nuggies to all of the ones standing around me before standing and clapping my hands to let Eden know I wanted to hold her. She leaned toward me, and Courtney and I made the exchange. Cora and the boys ran back in to the living room, and we followed them.

"Hey Ivy!" Shug called.

Everyone else yelled as well, and I said, "Hey!" to all of them at once.

"Your mom took me by your house today," Aunt Jane said, reaching out for a hug when I came near to her. "They've gotten a lot done since the last time I saw it."

I nodded, hugging three others that were in my vicinity at the edge of the kitchen. One of them was my mother, and when I hugged her, Eden leaned in like she wanted to stay with her. I kissed her cheek as I passed her to my mom.

"The contractor said it would just be a couple more months," I said, responding to Aunt Jane.

"You can almost count on doubling that," Daniel said.

I squinted at him, and he smiled and lifted his hands in surrender. "I'm just being realistic," he said. "I went over there a couple of days ago. They're staying busy, but you've still got electrical, and trim, and floors. You don't want them to rush, anyway. It's a good thing they're taking their time."

"I know," I said. "I'm not in a hurry. I've gotten used to eating Mom's cooking."

"You can still come eat once you move in," Mom said, feeding Eden a tiny bite of bread with her fingers.

I walked toward the stove to see what Shug was cooking. "Smells good," I said.

"Just some pork roast and potatoes," she said.

I leaned in behind her, staring into the pot and taking a big whiff. "I can't wait. I'm starving." I started to walk off, but she stretched out to kiss me, and I offered her my cheek. "Thanks for cooking," I said.

"My pleasure, baby girl. How was your week?"

"Busy. Good, but busy. "We got the cement poured for the basketball court two days ago."

"That's exciting," Shug said.

I nodded. "Some kids came and put their handprints in it."

"Oh, no, what'd you do?" Shug asked.

"I'm leaving it," I said. "The guys said they could fill it in, but it's on the edge and it's not bothering anything, so I decided leave it." I shrugged. "It's something I would have done if I saw some wet cement."

"You *did* do it," Mom said. "You put your hands *and* your feet in the slab we poured for the shed."

I laughed as I remembered doing that.

"Ivy was all about vandalism," Owen said. "She wrote her name in bubble letters under my desk and under a shelf in my closet."

Dad came into the kitchen, smiling and shaking his head. "I've found that little girl's signature in about twenty different places in the house," he said. "I went to fix a hinge on a cabinet the other day, and there it was, plain as day on the inside edge of the cabinet door, I-V-Y in black marker."

Everyone laughed, and I smiled and shrugged innocently. I found a spot to lean against the counter at the edge of the kitchen near the drink station. Shug had an area set up with a pitcher of sweet tea, a pitcher of water, a two-liter of Sprite, and a stack of plastic cups. There was a Sharpie near the cups, and everyone had another laugh when Mom told me to write my name on my cup.

I poured myself some iced tea, and as I was setting the pitcher down, a stack of papers caught my eye. Shug and Doozy had a small desk at the end of their kitchen, near the place where she had the drinks set up. It was a catchall and often contained their mail, their keys, Shug's purse, and anything else that would fit on it.

There was a stack of papers sitting on the edge, and I blinked as I stared at it. It was some official paperwork for the motorcycle company. I knew this because the logo was front and center.

It wasn't the logo that caught my eye, though. It was the writing underneath it. I would know it anywhere. Straight as an arrow, perfectly neat, block print—all caps. It even had the right kind of "E's"... the ones where the top line was a little too short and didn't quite touch the vertical line.

Chapter 11

A great number of bodily sensations happened all at once.

My heart began racing.

My eyes burned and blurred.

I felt a jittery, fluttering sensation in my chest like I couldn't catch my breath. I experienced a burst of adrenaline, and I was doing nothing but standing still.

I was stunned and confused as I stared down at the paper. It had been over a year since I had found that note in the front seat of my car, but I had looked at it what must have been a hundred times. I read it every day for the first month, and since then, I had read it as needed for strength and encouragement, or simply to put a smile on my face. I thought of it as *lovely* and *excellent* because reading it always made me think of that verse, which brought those words to mind. That being said, I had read that dang letter enough times to know the handwriting—the perfect, all-caps handwriting with the tell-tale "E's".

Why was the handwriting on this Bishop Motorcycles paperwork? Had my father written the letter? That thought gave me the weirdest feeling. Had my dad even known about Derek when I got that letter? No, Kade was the only person I had told.

I experienced a rush of emotions as I blinked at it. *What was this, anyway?* It seemed to be a cover letter of some sort. It contained serial numbers along with surface level information about a motorcycle—a new model maybe.

Courtney asked me a question about work, and I answered it. I was entirely preoccupied, but I did my best to engage with her.

Had my father written that letter? I thought back to it. Things like *'you deserve someone who would never betray you'*, would be something he would say, but other parts, like *'maybe forgiveness is the route you should take'*—that was not something my dad would say if he knew what had happened. In fact, now that I was thinking about it, I remembered his reaction a few days later when I told him. I remembered how enraged he was at Derek. *Had he been pretending that whole time?*

I thought about sifting through the pages to see if I could see more, but I had never taken the liberty of going through my family's personal things, even if they were sitting out in plain sight. There was only one thing for me to do. I had to ask someone about it.

Shug was busy talking to Taylor about her pork roast recipe, so I glanced around for other options. My grandfather had gone into the living room, and I walked in there as casually as possible. I still felt breathless, shaken, and utterly confused.

"Hey Dooz," I said, calling him the shortened version of his name.

"Hey baby," he said.

He put his arm around me, rubbing my shoulder and smiling at me as if he was happy that I had walked over there to stand next to him. I started to make small talk with him so that it didn't seem like I was anxious, but I was just too anxious to pretend I wasn't anxious.

"Hey, what is that over there on the desk?" I asked.

"What is it, baby?" he asked, looking around curiously.

I pointed toward the catchall in the kitchen. "There's some papers in there," I said. "It's Bishop stuff." I glanced at him, and he squinted curiously as he regarded the desk, looking like he was trying to figure out what I was talking about. "There's a whole stack of papers on the desk," I continued. "It looks like some information about a motorcycle or something."

He took a second to think about it, and then he shook his head like he just wasn't sure. "Why don't you bring it to me?" he said.

I flinched, starting to take off to the kitchen in order to retrieve the papers, but he gave my shoulders a squeeze.

"Oh, oh, oh, I think I know what you're talking about," he said. "That's that new model. It's the contract on that new one, the, uh, Ace. We're gonna make the Ace LT and MT models," he added with a smile.

"Well, who, uh, who wrote on it?" I asked. "On the front of the paper."

I felt so awkward asking that question. It was something I would've never normally noticed or asked about.

"Whatcha mean?" he asked, sweetly curious, but having no idea what I was asking. He was trying his best, but he simply wasn't answering me quickly enough. I motioned with my hand in the air like I was holding a pen and writing with it.

"The handwriting," I said "There's handwriting on the front of that paperwork. It's printed. It's just capital letters. Who wrote that?"

"Oh, that must have been, uh, Luke. If we're talking about the same thing. He's the one who designed those bikes. That's why it's called the LT, for London Town. He lives over there in London. He designed a MT model with some modifications. MT is for Memphis Town." Doozy smiled as if this detail pleased him. "That one's more of a ladies' bike—a little smaller than the LT. They're both real nice. I think they're gonna be top sellers for us next year."

I really couldn't even hear or comprehend the things he was saying. I had stopped listening after he said the word Luke. *Was he talking about Jolene's brother?* My mind was racing as I tried to remember the details of getting that note. Luke had been at my house when everything went down with Derek, but

110

he didn't know about it. There was no way he could've…

"He had the choice between a cash prize and commission from the models sold. He opted for the commission." Doozy smiled and gestured toward the desk. "That's what that contract's all about. Your mama helped our lawyers draw it up. He's smart. If that bike does as well as I think it will, that boy's about to get rich."

"Are you talking about Jolene's brother?" I asked, beginning to physically shake. I was breathless and my voice came out too high-pitched.

He stared down at me with a little grin as he nodded. "He won that contest," he said. "There were three finalists, but it was really down to him and this boy in L.A. who designed a big cruiser." He shook his head. "We didn't even know who the designers were when we chose the winner. It was unbiased. It was a total coincidence that Wes's wife was related to the winner." He grinned. "Your dad said he remembered him saying he was gonna win it."

"So, for sure that's his handwriting on those papers?" I asked.

"I think so," he said. "If we're thinking of the same thing. Why?"

"Oh, no reason. I just thought I recognized it and I… I thought maybe dad wrote it."

Doozy shook his head. "I don't think so, baby. Not if you're talking about that contract over there on the desk."

"Okay, y'all can come pray and make plates!" Shug yelled from the kitchen.

Doozy gave my shoulders another squeeze, assuming we'd go into the kitchen with everybody else. I smiled at him, and we made or way in that direction. Everyone bowed their heads, and Doozy blessed our meal, thanking God for food, and family, and the opportunity to share a life together.

People lined up in the kitchen and began making their own plates just as soon as he finished. I was still confused, trying to reconcile the similarities in handwriting from someone who didn't even know what happened with Derek and me.

"Is this what you were talking about?" Doozy asked, pointing at the stack of papers on the desk.

I was glad he drew attention to it. I wanted to ask about it again, but I didn't want to be obvious.

"Yes sir," I said, joining him casually. "I love that handwriting. I wish my handwriting was that good."

Shelby was standing close by when I said that, and she said something about changing her own handwriting when she was in her twenties. I responded to her and we had a little exchange, but I was totally focused on trying to get another glimpse of the paperwork.

"Can I look at it?" I asked.

Doozy nodded. "You're welcome to look at it, sweetie, but there's no picture of the bike in there.

It's just the contract and his bank information and everything."

"That's that Ace model coming out next season," Owen said, coming to stand next to us as he moved up in line.

"It's gonna sell like hotcakes," Dad said, looking over his shoulder. "It was really no contest between him and the other finalists. They were good, but we were almost unanimous voting for this one."

"Jolene's gonna be excited when she hears," I said, trying to act nonchalant.

"Oh, she already knows," Doozy said. "The contest was over a month ago."

"She was thrilled," Dad added. "Her brother flew over here to celebrate."

"When? He came over here? When was that? Recently?"

"Not *here*," Mom said, overhearing us and offering an explanation. "He came to the U.S., but not to Memphis. He met Wes and Jo a few weeks back when Wes was playing on the East Coast. He and Jolene have family in Philadelphia, so he flew in to meet them there. I think he wanted to see Wes play and catch up with their grandparents."

I felt frustrated that no one had thought to tell me that. But then again, why would they? I had gone to see Wes play in California and I didn't call Luke and tell him. Plus, I had been really busy with work and there were a lot of details I missed hearing about because of that.

113

I thumbed through the paperwork even though it was really none of my business. I had to see more of that handwriting just to make sure. It was, no doubt-no question, the same handwriting that was on my note.

My heart felt funny because of it.

I remembered how I felt during those first weeks—I felt like I could be in love with the person who wrote it. I even tried to make myself be attracted to Kade.

Then, I thought about Luke.

I pictured his face, his handsome face with that gorgeous mouth and those dark eyes. I remembered conversations we had and how I loved his kind, forgiving spirit, and his grit and determination. He was funny and smart and everything I should have been looking for in a man. I thought of the way my heart sped up when he brushed up against me and how I had to will myself not to look at him, lest I fall into temptation. I suddenly had the feeling that I missed out on something great by not falling for Luke.

Then I remembered that photograph of him with his girlfriend. The image of it flashed through my mind, and I felt nauseated. All of a sudden, Shug's pork roast didn't smell very appetizing. I was shaken to my very core—unsettled to say the least. I could not rest or think of anything else until I found out for sure if Luke was the one who had written that note.

"I'll be right back," I said to no one in particular.

There were so many people around and so much commotion that no one really cared that I was walking away. They just assumed that I was going to use the restroom. I went down the hall and into the spare bedroom where I took out my phone and dialed Jolene's number.

I held the phone to my ear, praying she would answer. Usually, we communicated with texts, so I wasn't sure. It was the fourth ring when she finally picked up. I thought it was going to her voicemail, but then I heard her voice.

"Hey Ivy, what's up?" she said.

Adrenaline was coursing through me, and I paced the floors wondering what in the world I was going to say to her.

I should have made a plan.

"Hey, what are y'all doing?" I asked.

"Just about to get some dinner," she said. "We're eating with Uncle Gray's family, and then they're all coming to the show."

"Aw, that's cool," I said. "Tell them all 'hi' for me."

"We will."

I was going to ask her how they were doing or how she was feeling with the pregnancy, but I couldn't resist getting right to the point.

"I just heard about your brother winning that contest," I said.

"Oh, yeah, isn't that awesome? He was so excited."

"Doozy said it's a nice bike," I said.

"I knew he'd win," she said. "He's talented and he's really passionate about motorcycles."

"Mom said he met y'all in Philly to celebrate," I said. "I've been so busy with work that I didn't hear about it."

"I know," Jolene said. "Your mom keeps us posted on all the work you're doing. I know you've been busy. We're all really proud of you."

There was no tactful way to ask, but I had so many questions just bubbling up, ready to come out. *How was Luke? What was he doing? Does he have a girlfriend? Was he capable of writing a magical note and leaving it in my car?* I had to know. I couldn't fake disinterest any longer.

"JoJo, I think Luke might have left something at the house when he came to visit," I said. "I was wondering if I could get his phone number from you so I can call him and see."

"Sure," she said. "I'll text you his number when we hang up."

I was almost sure she'd ask what he left or question me further, but she didn't.

"Thank you," I said. "Hug my brother and yourself for me, and my little niece or nephew, and tell Uncle Gray's family we said 'hi'."

"I will. We miss you guys. We'll be home next week."

"I can't wait," I said.

We exchanged 'I love yous' and 'goodbyes' before hanging up.

Seconds later, I got a text with Luke's contact information.

Chapter 12

I didn't hesitate.

I didn't Google the time difference or anything. That didn't even cross my mind.

I clicked on Jolene's text, saw Luke's contact information, and pressed the 'call' button. It was only after his phone rang three times that I remembered that it might be in the middle of the night over there.

"Hello?"

His deep voice answered, and my stomach tensed up at the sound of it. I was already nauseated, and now I was short of breath. I should have given myself a second to think of what I was going to say before I called. I could barely breathe.

"Hello," I said. "I'm sorry. Is it the middle of the night over there?"

"It's midnight," he said.

I could hear some commotion, and I wondered where he was. Also, it sounded like he had a British accent.

"Why, what time is it where you are?" he asked.

He definitely had an accent.

"Six," I said, hesitantly.

"In the morning?" he asked.

"Evening," I said.

"Where are you calling from, exactly?"

"The United States." I answered vaguely since I was relatively sure I wasn't talking to Luke, and I didn't want to give my location. "I'm trying to reach Luke Wright."

"What's Luke doing getting a call from the United States?" the person asked, as if calling into the room.

"It's probably his sister," I heard another man say.

Then I heard, "What are you doing answering my phone?"

There was some rustling around, and then there he was.

"Hello?" he asked.

No accent.

It was Luke; I knew it.

I was out of my head with nerves.

I paced the floor.

"Luke?" I said.

"Yeah, hang on. Let me... Is this Jo?"

"No, it's not. Is it a bad time?"

"No. It's fine. Who is this?"

"It's Ivy Bishop."

"Really?" I could hear the smile in his voice, and it made me smile.

"Yes really."

"How are you? Is everything okay with my sister?"

"Yeah, she's fine. She's good. I just got off the phone with her."

"Are you okay?" he asked.

"I'm fine."

I continued to hear commotion.

"Where are you?" I asked.

"One of our customers owns a pub over here in Chelsea. A bunch of us came over here to hang out and listen to some music. What's going on? It's good to hear from you."

"I worried, after I called, that you might be sleeping," I said, since I was a huge, nervous dork.

"Not on a Friday night," he said.

There was a smile in his voice, and I felt jealous that he was doing anything but hanging out with me on a Friday night. I felt an astounding amount of nerves and butterflies just from the sound of his voice.

I continued to pace. I could hear him changing locations. The commotion died down. I could still hear sounds, but they were quieter.

"I'm stepping outside," he said. "I could hardly hear you in there." He took a deep breath. "Am I dreaming, or did you say this was Ivy Bishop?" he asked.

"You're not dreaming," I said. I was so excited to talk to him that I felt as though my face could crack to pieces with a smile. I opened my mouth really big to stretch it out, trying to get myself together enough to speak like a rational person.

"What are you doing calling me, Ivy Bishop?"

"I, uh, had, I had a question for you."

"Ask away," he said.

Again, I could hear him smiling. His deep confident voice sent chills up my spine. I was nervous to the point of breathlessness, but I spoke anyway.

"Luke, did, uh, you leave a... was there a... the day you left... did you happen to leave... a note?"

A long pause followed my question.

Maybe it was just a few seconds, but to me, it felt like a lifetime. I was just about to ask if he was still there when he answered.

"I did," he said.

My heart absolutely hammered in my chest.

I let out a long sigh.

"Was that a bad choice?" he asked reluctantly.

"I thought it was Kade who wrote that this whole time."

He let out a little laugh on a breath. "It was me," he said. "I hope that wasn't overstepping. I just wanted you to know that—"

"It wasn't," I said. "Overstepping, I mean."

I took another breath, still pacing the bedroom absentmindedly.

"I don't want to get you in trouble with your girlfriend by calling you at midnight or saying this or anything, but that letter... Luke, it was, uh, really... special to me. It, uh, helped me in ways... (sigh) Anyway, I just wanted you to know that it helped me. I wanted to say thanks. I wish I would have known it was you who wrote it so I could've thanked you sooner."

121

"You're very welcome, Ivy. I meant all of it. You're a remarkable woman. It was difficult to see you hurting that day."

I saw something in the hall, and I looked up to find that my mom had come to check on me. I smiled at her and held out a finger to let her know I'd join them in a minute. She smiled and nodded, disappearing again.

"How did you know?" I asked. "How did you know what happened?"

"I went into your room to check on you, and I heard you talking to your friend. I didn't mean to listen to your conversation. I thought you had invited me into the room, and I was already inside before I realized you were talking to someone else. I felt really bad for listening. That's why I didn't sign the note."

I was quiet for several seconds, thinking about that note and all the things it said.

"That's why I assumed your note was from Kade," I said. "Because he was the only person I told."

I heard him take a breath. "I'm sorry."

"Don't be. I'm glad I figured it out. It's actually a relief. I knew something didn't add up. The Kade I know wasn't the same Kade who wrote that letter."

"You're right about that," he said with a laugh.

"I tried to love him," I said.

I did my best to stop myself from saying that, but the words just came out without my permission.

I was wrecked with nerves, and it just came out. I almost physically choked when I said it. The words literally got stuck in my throat.

"You what?" he asked.

"Love him," I said. "I tried to love Kade. I was so moved by the note that I tried to see him like that."

"What? Are you messing with me, Ivy?"

"No, I'm not. I'm serious. I thought it was Kade who wrote it, and I tried to fall in love with him because of it."

"You're kidding me."

"No, I'm not."

"Are you seeing him now?"

"No," I said. "Like I said, the Kade I know wasn't the same Kade who wrote that letter. As much as I tried to imagine he was, he just wasn't."

He let out a long sigh like he was a tire being deflated. "Thank God, Ivy. Because I seriously don't know what I would do if you were calling me right now telling me that you were with in love with some guy because of a note *I* wrote. I'm already tripped out enough that you're calling in the first place. You're the last person on Earth I expected to hear from tonight."

"I just found out you won that contest," I said. "I saw the contract sitting on Doozy's desk. That's how I knew it was you. I saw the handwriting."

"Oh, my gosh, are you serious?"

"Yes."

"That's unbelievable."

"It is to me, too."

"I can't believe you recognized the handwriting."

"I can't believe you wrote that letter."

We were both quiet for a few long seconds.

"Congratulations on winning that contest, by the way," I added. "Doozy said you designed a nice bike."

"Thank you," he said. "It's definitely a dream come true. They should be out next winter."

"I'm gonna have to get one," I said.

"You'd look good on that MT."

His words caused a gut-clenching sensation to happen inside me.

"You shouldn't give me those types of compliments," I said.

"Why not? You would look good on it. It's just a fact."

"But your girlfriend might not be too happy about you stating such a fact."

"That's the second time you mentioned my nonexistent girlfriend, Ivy. You better be careful. I'm gonna start thinking you don't want me to have one."

I had to bite my lip to keep myself from giggling. I stopped in my tracks and my toes curled as I stared at the floor.

"I don't… you… I thought you… what happened to your, that girl you were dating. I thought you were dating someone."

"We broke up about a year ago. I've dated like three other girls since her, but none of them..."

"What? None of them what?"

"None of them worked out."

"Oh. That's good. I mean, not that there were three girls, but that there aren't... anymore girls."

"Why do you care so much about my love life, Ivy?"

"Because I do," I said, since I couldn't think of anything else to say.

"Hang on one second. *Just go ahead,*" he said, talking to someone else. "*Just play without me. I don't know. Five minutes. Maybe an hour. I'm on the phone.* Okay, I'm back," he said, talking to me again.

"I don't mean to keep you," I said.

"You don't?"

"No. Do you need to go?"

"What I need, is to continue having this conversation with you," he said.

"You do?"

"Yes, I do. I'm still waiting for you to tell me why you keep asking about my girlfriend."

"Because I don't want you to have one," I said. "Is that what you want to hear?"

"Yes, it is," he said. "Is it the truth? Or are you just telling me what I want to hear?"

"I'm the one who called you, Luke. I'm the one who hasn't been able to breathe or think straight since I saw that handwriting on my granddad's desk. When you were here, I, I had such a good time with you. I liked you so much, but I had just started dating Derek and I knew that... I don't know. You had a girlfriend, too. Neither of us could really... But I saw you like that. I really did. I felt something. I was tempted to... I don't know. Maybe it was just me, but I feel like things would've been different if we weren't... I liked you, Luke. If I would have known it was you who wrote that note, things might have turned out a lot different."

He let out a long, frustrated sigh—one with a groan attached to it. I could imagine him rubbing his face with his hand.

"Well, now you know it," he said. "I wrote it. I meant it. And I felt something for you, too, Ivy. Why do you think I left her when I got back here? Even though nothing happened between us, I felt guilty because of how much I wanted it to. I left a piece of my heart over there in Memphis."

"You left a piece of paper here, too," I said. "Only you didn't sign your name on it so I had no idea who it belonged to."

"Something I really regret, in hindsight."

"You should really come pick it up," I said.

It was a straight-up proposition, a shameless proposition, and my heart was beating so fast it felt like it might explode.

"The piece of paper, or my heart?" he asked.

"Neither one," I said breathlessly. "I regret saying that. I don't think I would give either of them back."

"Then, why should I come? Sounds like a wasted trip if you're not gonna give me the goods you promised."

"I probably shouldn't have said you should come pick it up. That was the wrong thing for me to offer. I should have phrased it more carefully. I should have said you could come bring me the rest of it."

He cleared his throat. "I'm fairly certain you're not referring to the piece of paper right now."

"No, I'm not."

There was a long pause.

"Tell me what you're saying, Ivy. Say it in plain English."

My heart pounded so relentlessly that I thought it might burst.

"I want to see you, Luke. Really bad. I wish you were standing in the same room with me right now. I'm frustrated that there's a whole ocean between us."

"I don't even know what to say," he said. "Who am I talking to? Is this really Ivy Bishop? The girl from Memphis? I feel like I'm trippin' right now."

"How do you think I feel? I've been in love with a note for over year, and now I find out that I already kinda liked the guy who wrote it."

He laughed. "If I come over there, Ivy. I just want to give you a fair warning that I'm probably not gonna wanna just be your friend."

"That's good, Luke, because a friendship's not really what I'm offering you."

Chapter 13

I was still in the guest bedroom, talking to Luke on the phone when Kip ran in, followed by Cora. She was chasing him with a plastic hammer, and he ran in, screaming.

Once he was fully in the room, he turned and clinched his fists, yelling at her to, "*Stoooop!*" His fists were clinched and he leaned forward when he yelled, looking like a roaring bear who was standing his ground.

Startled by his sudden anger, Cora flinched and made a pouty face. Her chin quivered, and her face crumpled, and Courtney appeared in the doorway just in time to see Cora's pitiful face turn toward her.

"What in the world?" she said, stooping over to pick up Cora. "Kip what did you do to your cousin?"

"Nothin', " he said. "She was de one chasin' me wif du hamma."

Courtney looked at me, and I nodded, confirming Kip's story. "He yelled for her to stop, and I think it scared her," I said.

Courtney noticed that I had my phone to my ear, and she apologized for their intrusion. "Y'all let Aunt Ivy have some peace and quiet in here," she said, ushering them out.

"I'll be out in a minute," I told her. "Sorry," I said, once they walked out.

"Sounds like you have a lot going on over there."

"It was the kids," I said. "We're over here eating dinner at Shug and Doozy's. Cora came in, chasing Kip with a hammer."

He laughed. "Never a dull moment," he said.

"Nope."

"I bet they're getting big."

"They are," I said. "Babies everywhere. And Shelby's pregnant again. Jolene, too, but I guess you knew that already."

"Yeah. She wasn't showing when I saw her, but she said she's starting to now. Crazy to think that I'm gonna have a little niece or nephew."

"I know," I said. I had to stop myself from saying that he already had six of them and two more on the way, but then I realized that he didn't. Not yet, at least. I was instinctually assuming he was already mine and that my family was his family. So, funny. I really did feel like Luke already belonged with me— like he was already a part of me, and my heart knew it long before my brain did. I had a flashback of him wearing that Bishop hoodie. I remembered feeling like he was already a Bishop. I just didn't understand, at that point, that he was supposed to be linked through me. I felt a wave of excitement and anticipation because of it. I really couldn't wait to see him again.

We had already been on the phone for about a half an hour, and I knew both of us needed to get back to what we were doing before I called. I couldn't, however, let him go without making some concrete plans.

"When do you think you can come?" I asked.

"I was just trying to think about that," he said. "I've got a restoration starting next week. The customer specifically asked for me to oversee it. But after I get it started, I think I should be able to—"

"That's too long," I said cutting him off. "I thought you were gonna say tomorrow—tonight even."

He let out a little laugh like he thought I might be joking, and my heart felt like it was breaking. I was completely unable to be patient about this, and I was amazed and probably a little heartbroken that he, apparently, had all the patience in the world.

Both of us were quiet for a few seconds, and then he said, "Were you being serious?"

"Yes," I said, my heart pounding. In the back of my mind, I knew how selfish it was of me to assume that he could just drop everything and take a spur of the moment trip to another continent, but I rarely paid attention to the back of my mind. It was the front of my mind that was telling me I needed to see him *now*. Even tomorrow felt like too long, much less days or weeks.

"If you can't come here sooner than that, I'm going there."

"You have even more responsibilities than I do, Ivy."

(Just before the kids had barged into the room, Luke and I were talking about my work at the nonprofit, so he knew how busy I had been lately.)

I honestly didn't care about my responsibilities—that's how desperate I was to see him. I knew someone would step up to pick up my slack if I had to take off for a few days.

"I don't care," I said. "Someone will cover for me."

"Ivy, are you that anxious to see me?" he asked.

"Yes, Luke, I am."

I didn't care that I sounded desperate.

I was desperate.

Talking to him and hearing his voice made me absolutely yearn to see him. I ached for it. Knowing that he was the one who wrote the letter had me beside myself, and remembering how attracted I was to him didn't help matters.

I had to see him.

I felt like I needed to leave that instant.

He took a deep breath. "Ivy this is all so... I mean, I didn't even expect to hear from you tonight, let alone find out that you want to see me."

"I'm sorry if it feels like I'm rushing you. I'm not trying to—"

"No. Don't apologize. I just had no idea that I'd be having this conversation."

"I didn't either," I said. "But here we are."

"Yep. Here we are."

"Do you want to see me, Luke?"

A few seconds of silence passed.

"More than I can say, Ivy."

I could hear the sincerity in his tone, and I felt a weight off my chest because of it.

"I want to see you, too. I can't wait, though, Luke. If you need to stay and work or whatever, then I'll go to you. I don't want to wait another week. I'll go to London."

Again, Luke was quiet on the other end.

"Luke?"

"Ivy, I feel like I'm dreaming right now, or maybe I'm crazy. Do you seriously want to see me bad enough to drop everything and come over here?"

"I will leave here and go to the airport," I said.

"Oh, Ivy." His deep voice came out unsteady. "You're making my heart... I can't even tell you how much I... Ivy, I'll come there. I'll come to you. Amos and Randall can cover for me at work. Just say the word, and I'll go to my apartment and—"

"The word," I said, not needing to hear any more. "I'm saying it. Whatever words you need to hear, I'm saying them. Drop everything, Luke. Get here. Do it as fast as you can, please."

"Okay," he said resolutely. "Let me see what I can do. I'll call you back in just a little bit."

"Tonight?" I asked.

"Yes, tonight," he said, amusement in his voice.

"Okay," I said.

I wanted so badly to tell him I loved him. The words were on the very tip of my tongue, and I had to make myself hold them back. I knew in my heart that I loved him, and it took all of my self-control to refrain from telling him.

"Okay, so I'll talk to you in a little bit."

"Okay," I repeated. "But you're coming, right?"

"Yes, Ivy, I'm coming." I still heard that smile in his voice, and I imagined what he looked like. I could see him on a London sidewalk, outside a pub, holding his phone to his ear and smiling. He was smiling because of me, and I felt all warm and fuzzy because of it.

"I like you, Luke," I said, since I couldn't let myself say the other "L" word even though I really wanted to.

"Good, because I'm about to fly across the world to come see you."

I was so elated by his words that I stood next to the bed and collapsed onto it, landing flat on my back. I scrunched up my face, feeling as though I needed to let out a silent scream.

"What was that?" he asked, hearing the whooshing sounds of my collapse.

"Nothing," I said. "I was just sitting down."

"I'll call you in a little while," he said.

"Okay. Bye."

"Bye, Ivy."

I could hear that same smile in his voice when he said it, and it caused a wave of love and desire to crash over me.

I hung up my phone, but right after I did, I let out a squeal of delight, shivering at the thought that I would see him soon. I was lying flat on my back on Shug's guest bed when I did that, so I didn't see anyone standing at the door.

It was Doozy, but I didn't know it until he said, "You okay?"

"Yes sir," I said, sitting straight up. Try as I might, I could not wipe a huge grin off of my face.

"Looks like you got some good news," he said, smiling back at me.

"I did."

"Somethin' you wanna share?"

"Luke's coming."

He pulled back, regarding me with a somewhat confused look. "Luke?"

I nodded.

"You mean the same boy from London? The one from the contest?"

"He's not a boy, Doozy." I tried, but I literally could not stop smiling.

"Ohhhh, no," he said, giving me a sideways glance.

My smile grew even bigger when he said that, and I put my fists in front of my face to hide it.

"Did you come in here and call him when I told you he won that contest?"

I nodded. "But not because he won. I mean, I'm happy that he won, but that's not why I called him."

"And you say he's coming to Memphis?"

I nodded.

He tilted his head at me. "To visit or to stay?"

I shrugged and shook my head. "I have no idea. To stay, I hope. I don't know. I just asked him to get on a plane, and he said he would. That's as far as we got."

Doozy made a thoughtful expression as if he was really trying to analyze what I was saying. I could tell his wheels were really turning.

"I was just remembering... I don't know if it means anything, but after the contest was over, Jack told me that boy had originally turned in the bike designs as the Ace and the Ivy. Jack had to call him and get him to rename them because we've already had an Ivy model, back in the sixties. Plus, Jack thought he was trying to get my vote by naming his bike after my wife. They settled on the LT and MT before we ever looked at them. I didn't even know any of that happened until the contest was over and Jack told me that story."

Doozy shifted and gave me a long, hard look.

"I guess maybe he wasn't calling it Ivy for your grandmother, was he?"

I shook my head, my heart still hammering in my chest. "No sir, I don't think he was."

"Does your dad know you've been talking to him?"

"I haven't. We haven't talked to each other since he came here a year ago. There was a note, and... it's a long story. There was a misunderstanding, and I didn't know it was him who… but it all makes sense. It really does. It makes so much sense now."

"I don't know if I've ever seen you grinning like this, Ivy."

"You haven't," I said. "I'm pretty sure you haven't."

"So, you really like this young man?"

I hesitated, because I wasn't sure what words I could say to convey how very much I did. "So much," I said, hoping that was enough.

"Well, for what it's worth, he's an extremely determined person. Randall called your father after he won to tell us we had made the right decision—he said the boy's really gifted. I knew someone special had made those designs. I don't know if I've seen that kind of creativity and ingenuity in a design since…"

"Yours?" I guessed.

He laughed. "That's what I was thinking, but then I realized how bad it sounded for me to say that. I was trying to pay him a compliment, not myself."

I reached out and hugged my grandfather, and he hugged me back. "Comparing him to you, Dooz, is the biggest compliment he could ever get."

"What do you want, you precious angel?" he asked in a cooing tone, like he was about to get out his checkbook and buy me the whole world if I asked for it.

I laughed. "I really do just want him to get here," I said since it was honestly the only thing on my mind.

He shrugged. "Well, call him and tell him his plane ticket's on the company. Your mama's probably got a company card in her wallet. Just ask her for it, and pay for his ticket on that."

Chapter 14

I got a call from Luke two hours later. It was nearly nine o'clock my time, which meant it was just about three in the morning in London. The later it got, the more I thought he wouldn't call, but my phone finally rang.

"Hello?" I said.

"Hey," he said.

"You sound tired."

"I am. I'm sorry that took so long. I was depending on someone else for a ride, and we ended up having to go half-way across London to take home his… anyway, I avoided killing him and finally made it back to my place. I'm here now."

I wished I was sitting right next to him. "You probably need to get some rest," I said. I wanted him to insist that he didn't need rest and tell me that he was leaving for the airport momentarily.

"I searched flights from my phone while we were driving around," he said.

I bit my lip, feeling so excited. "And?"

"There are tons of options," he said. "I mean, there's a flight leaving like every two hours or so. Did you think you wanted me to come as early as tomorrow? I guess that's technically today since it's morning over here."

"Luke."

"What?"

"Please get here as fast as you can."

"I'm looking at it right now. It seems like the absolute earliest one would be getting into Memphis about five o'clock tomorrow afternoon. That one leaves in just a few hours. I think that would give me time to pack a few things and get out the door."

"Please take it. Is that the earliest?"

"There's one that gets me there a couple hours earlier, but it's like double the price, and I didn't—"

"I'm paying. We're paying. Doozy is. He said he'd pay. I was gonna tell you that. I have the company credit card right here. I was actually gonna ask if I could just call and make the reservation for you. Would the one that gets here earlier still give you enough time to get to the airport?"

"That one actually doesn't leave until 7am. It's got one stop instead of two. It gives me an extra hour on my end."

"Okay, that's the one I'll get. Just take a screen shot of it and send it to me. I'll take care of paying for it."

It was quiet on the other end.

"Luke?"

"I don't know when to get the return flight. We haven't talked about that. Everything's just so fast that…"

He trailed off, and my heart dropped.

"However long you want," I said. "Three days, five days, forever."

I heard him let out a little laugh. "What do you think?"

"I think you already know what I think," I said.

"What?"

"Luke, I really don't care. I'm just trying to get you here. I'll worry about talking you into staying later. As far as I'm concerned, you can get a one-way."

Again, he paused, thinking.

The silence was deafening.

"Just get a one-way," he said finally. "It'll be cheaper that way, and I can just buy the one-way back after I have time to figure out what day."

"You want to stay," I said, grinning.

"First, I have to get there," he said.

"Okay, I'm hanging up. Text me with that flight information, and I'll buy your ticket right now."

"Ivy?"

"What?"

"Never mind."

"What?" I said.

"Nothing."

"Tell me."

"Nothing. I'm just tired. I was just wondering… it crossed my mind to wonder… what if I get there, and things aren't what you expected? I mean, so much time has passed. What if I look different than you thought? What if you feel differently about—"

"What if you feel differently about me?" I asked. "What if you see me and you don't like me anymore?"

"That's not possible," he said.

"That's how I feel about you," I said. "Please just get off the phone with me so I can buy the ticket and you can get here. Then I can show you what I'm talking about."

He laughed. "Okay," he said.

I purchased a one-way ticket for Luke.

I was in constant contact with him until we got it squared away. I had to have more information than just his name to reserve the tickets, so I called him back and he stayed on the phone with me while I dealt with the airline from the house phone.

I could hardly sleep that night knowing that he was on his way. I took out his letter and read it again. I was full of joy, knowing in my heart that the man who penned those words was the man intended for me. He was the one who had been chosen for me, there was no doubt in my mind.

The following day was Saturday, so there was no tutoring at the nonprofit. It was open from 10-2 for students who wanted to come in and study on their own or just needed a place to hang out. I had one other person there with me, so I left a little early and asked them to lock up.

I still had a couple of months to go at my parents' house while my own place was being completed. My mom was home when I got there, and we talked while I changed and freshened up. I hadn't yet clued in my mother on how very much I knew I loved Luke, but she could tell something was different with me. It was evident by the way she looked at me that she could tell I was a woman in love—it was almost as if she sympathized with me over it. Or maybe she just looked nostalgic because now all of her children had found their match. Either way, I could tell she knew how I felt even without me saying it.

I started to leave in such haste that I was about to pick him up on a motorcycle without any way to carry his bags. It was still early spring, but the day was warm enough to ride, and I was definitely in the mood.

"Why don't you let me follow you up there," Mom suggested. "I'll wait in the car and take his bags so y'all can ride the bike."

I took my mom up on her offer, and she followed me to the airport. I half expected her to want to come in. I thought I might have to break it to her that I wanted to greet Luke on my own, but it that wasn't necessary. She voluntarily remained in the car while I went inside.

Okay, so maybe I was a little impatient.

His flight was scheduled to arrive at 3:09 and I glanced at my phone when I made it to baggage claim, and it was 2:36. I sent my mom a text telling her I was sorry she had to wait so long, and she texted me back saying that I shouldn't worry about it, and that she was taking care of a few emails while she was sitting there.

I found a spot on a bench and fished a pair of earbuds out of my purse so that I could listen to music. I turned on a playlist with classics by Chuck Berry, Elvis, Etta James, Roy Orbison, Muddy Waters, Otis Redding, and of course there were a few songs on there by my Shug. I zoned out, getting lost in the music while I waited. I had Wes's new album on my Spotify, too, but I had already worn that out, and I was in the mood for blues classics, anyway. They always calmed me down.

At the moment, I happened to be listening to one that got me pumped instead of calming me down. It was *Something's Got a Hold on Me* by Etta James.

On this day, I happened to really identify with the lyrics, and I couldn't help myself from boogying to the music as I sat there on that bench. It started with simple facial expressions as I sang along— mouthing the words. I closed my eyes and listened to her belt out the passionate lyrics.

Oh, oh, sometimes I get a good feeling, yeah.
(yeah)
I get a feeling that I never, never, never, never, had before, no no.
(yeah)
I just wanna tell you right now that, uh, (oooh)
I believe, I really do believe, that…

Something's got a hold on me, yeah.
(Oh, it must be love.)
Oh, something's got a hold on me right now,
child.
(Oh, it must be love.)

Let me tell you now,
I've got a feeling,
I feel so strange,
Everything about me seems to have changed,
Step-by-step, I got a brand-new walk,
I even sound sweeter when I talk.

I said, oh, (oh), oh, (oh), oh, (oh), *oh!* (oh),
Hey, hey, yeah.
Oh, it must be love.

Let me tell you now,
Something's got a hold on me...

I was really into this song—so into it, that my simple facial expressions and lyric-mouthing had turned into more complex gestures. I had added toe and finger tapping, along with seat-shifting, and who knows what other wiggling and jiggling.

Etta James was passionate, and I knew every word and every beat of the song by heart. This, combined with the fact that I really and truly identified with these lyrics at the moment made it impossible for me to keep still.

It was somewhere near the end of the song when I felt two hands touch my shoulders. I jumped and gasped, and opened my eyes in utter shock, the earbuds flying out of my ears in the process.

Luke.

It was Luke.

He had touched me.

He was standing right in front of me, smiling sweetly, his dark eyes squinting with pure pleasure as he stared down at me. I jumped up, springing into his arms with no hesitation whatsoever, and he caught me, his chest vibrating with laughter at how quickly I had bolted out of my seat.

"I think your phone fell," he said.

"I don't care," I said, squeezing him tightly.

It was Luke. He was here. He had come for me. He was in Memphis, and he had come here for me— not to see his sister, or to build a motorcycle, but for me. I held onto him so tightly that I felt like our energy literally became one, our breathing fell into sync—like our bodies partially melted together as we were standing there.

Aside from that little glance when I first opened my eyes, I hadn't even seen his face. I knew, just from that quick scan, that he was everything I was expecting and more. He was even more handsome than I remembered. He was more of a man, too. I could even feel it by hugging him. He was thick and broad-chested, and this year that we had spent apart had done nothing but make him even more irresistible than he was before. I was smitten right down to my bones. My knees were weak, and I felt like I could just melt into his arms.

"What in the world were you listening to, Ivy?" he asked, without looking at me.

"Etta James," I said. "Why? Was I dancing?"

"Yes. I was watching you the whole way down the escalator. I kept thinking you'd open your eyes and look at me."

"You probably thought, *'who's that crazy girl, sitting there with her eyes closed'.*"

"I was actually thinking that you are the most beautiful, precious thing I have ever seen in my life. I can't think of a single person who could possibly look so lovely, sitting on a bench and wiggling around to music that only she could hear."

"Lovely," I said. "I like that word."

"You are lovely, Ivy."

I glanced up, but we were so close and he was so tall that all I could see was his neck. He was wearing a button-down shirt layered with a light jacket, and I loved how handsome and sharp he looked. He smelled clean and masculine just like I remembered, and my stomach clinched at the feeling of his arms around me.

He began to move, pulling back so that he could look down at me. I was in his arms. We were right up against each other. I was here—finally here, touching him. I could barely breathe.

I looked straight at his mouth, that mouth, the one with the gorgeous upper lip that came out over the bottom one. There it was, right in front of me, begging to be kissed. Only now I didn't have to be shy to look at it—now I could shamelessly check him out.

I peeled my arm away from his side and slid it between us so that I could reach up and touch him. Slowly, I brought my hand to his face, letting my fingertips touch his jaw before running up his cheek. I couldn't help it. I let my thumb touch the edge of his mouth—it was just that irresistible. I stood there and stared at him, and he did the same to me. We just gawked at each other as if we were the only two people in the airport.

Chapter 15

My heart was still pounding from Luke's shocking appearance. It probably wasn't only the shock of having him sneak up on me with my eyes closed. It was everything—having him here, being in his arms, and realizing that he was even better (more handsome, sweet, and wonderful) than I recalled.

"I didn't know your flight got here," I said, staring at him.

He grinned. "I know. I saw you not see me."

"I was listening to Etta James."

"I didn't mean to scare you."

"I can't believe you're here."

"You're the one who invited me," he said.

"I know, and you came." I smiled shyly. "You picked up and left London when I called."

"And I would do it again," he said, scanning my face. "I wish I could have gotten here sooner."

My fingertips were still lightly touching the side of his face. There was stubble on his jaw, and I loved the feel of it shifting, so I gently and slowly flexed my fingers.

"Luke." I didn't mean for it to, but my voice came out like a desperate whisper.

"Ivy," he said, answering me and holding me even more tightly around my waist.

"Your letter," I said.

The corner of his mouth lifted in a half smile. "That old thing?" he asked, casually.

I shook my head. "You have no idea what it meant. So much has happened to me since then—being okay with the breakup, and then the nonprofit and the house. I can't help but feel like I owe... I'm just so thankful for those things you wrote. They inspired me—they made me feel capable and worthy."

"You are capable and worthy, Ivy. It's almost kind of surreal for me to hear that my note somehow helped you see that. I thought I was being redundant when I wrote it. I almost didn't leave it."

My heart fell when he said that. In those split seconds, I imagined what it would have been like had I not found the note that morning. I imagined how differently things could've turned out. I realized I wouldn't be standing with him in this moment, and that was just completely unacceptable. I shivered at the thought of it, and he smiled and held me closer.

I repositioned my hands, holding him tightly around his waist again and snuggling even closer.

"You cold?"

"No. But if I say I am, will you kiss me?"

He grinned "You don't have to say that to get me to kiss you. You don't have to say anything."

We stood there, staring at each other. People were bustling about, getting their luggage, and walking past us. We didn't flinch. It was as if no one was even there. He looked a little different than I remembered—and in all the right ways. He was more of a man. I innately felt like he was able to care for me—protect me.

"Why aren't you doing it, then?" I whispered.

"Doing what?"

"Kissing me."

He scanned my face. "Ivy, am I awake right now? Am I even alive? This doesn't seem real."

I gave him a little nod. "Kiss me and find out." And just like that, he leaned down, closing the gap between our mouths, and letting his gorgeous, full lips fall gently onto mine.

Electricity.

My insides experienced a warm, zapping sensation that made my toes curl and my fists clinch. I stretched up, leaning into him. My knees were so weak, that I depended on him to help hold me up. His mouth tasted just like I thought it would. It was soft and warm, and his lips found their home on mine two, three, five, seven times, all with great tenderness. After what must have been ten soft kisses, Luke pulled back reluctantly, straightening his shoulders and staring off to the side as if he couldn't bear to do it again.

"I missed you," I said, squeezing him and wanting desperately to kiss him again.

"Ivy."

"What?"

He stared at me like he was searching for the right words. "I'm a man."

I grinned. "I know."

He looked at me thoughtfully as his chest rose and fell with gentle breaths. "And I think I might be more in love with you than any man has ever been with any woman. Ever."

Those words, coming out of his mouth, caused another wave of warm desire to wash over me. I squeezed my eyes shut tight for a second before looking at him again. "What's so wrong with that?" I whispered once I opened them.

"We're in an airport and if I kiss you the way I want to kiss you right now, we might end up on the news. We might cause a scene."

"I'm sure there's lots of kissing at the airport," I said, still wanting him to do it again.

He shook his head. "Not by men who are more in love than any man has ever been, ever."

I smiled. "How about just another little, baby one?"

He leaned in, putting his face closer to mine. His lips were only an inch or two away when he whispered to me. "Like this?" (kiss) It was so soft and sweet that I almost whimpered.

I nodded. "Again," I whispered. (kiss) This one lingered slightly longer, but it was still so soft and gentle.

He knew how to kiss me. He knew exactly what I wanted to feel—exactly what would make me weak with desire. I held him tightly around his waist, noticing for the first time, the feel of his back and sides under my arms, our skin was separated by layers of clothing, and still, I could feel his warmth and tightness, and the ridges of his muscles.

I had been so preoccupied that I was only now, for the first time, feeling that he had a bag strapped to his shoulder. It was hanging behind him, and I leaned over in his arms to try to catch a glimpse of it.

"I'm sorry. I didn't know you're holding a bag," I said. I glanced at the baggage carousel for his flight, which was already in motion. "We should probably look for your other stuff.

"This is all I have," he said.

"One carryon?" I asked.

My hands were already positioned behind him, so I grabbed the strap, and lifted it upward, testing the weight. "Oh, my goodness, Luke. This is heavy. I'm so sorry you've been standing here holding this."

He gave me an easy grin. "Ivy, I could hold about twenty of these if I had to right now. I'm pretty sure I could hold a bus on my back with you standing right here."

I smiled. "Speaking of bus, guess what I picked you up on?"

"Well, the fact that you said 'on' instead of 'in' would lead me to believe that it's not a car."

I shook my head. "It's not."

"What bike?" he asked, knowing that mine wasn't a two-seater.

"My dad's black one—well, one of his black ones. The one you took out last time you were here."

"That time, you weren't on it with me."

"Yeah, but this time, I will be."

"What are we waiting for?" he asked.

Luke held my hand on our way out of the airport. At first, we were just holding hands, joined by fingers that were laced together. But soon, that wasn't enough for me. I pulled his whole arm in front of my chest, gripping onto it and leaning against his shoulder as we walked.

We were in that same position when we made our way out to the parking lot. Luke had no idea my mom had followed me there, and even though he knew what she drove, it didn't sink in that she would be parked right next to me.

"Hey Luke," she said, opening her door when we made our way to the bike.

"Hey, Mrs. Bishop," he said, trying his best to hide his surprise.

"I forgot to tell you my mom came," I said as Mom came around to the back of the SUV. "She's gonna carry home your luggage."

"Please call me Rose, baby." She reached out for a hug, and I let go of Luke's hand so he could return it. "Oh, my goodness, you're bigger than my boys," she said with a groan as she wrapped her arms around him.

She pulled back and held him at arm's length, giving him a once-over before glancing at me. She

153

gave me a quick, conspiratorial smile that I knew meant he was really handsome. I shot her a super-fast silly face, wrinkling my nose.

"Is this all you have?" she asked.

"Yes, ma'am," he said.

She pushed the button to open the back hatch, and we all stood back while it swung upward. Luke assumed he should put his bag into the back, so he took it off his shoulder, and placed it securely in the corner. My mom reached out and patted his shoulder again, looking impressed by his stature.

"It really is good to see you again, Luke. I'm glad you came to see us."

"You have no idea how happy I am to be here. I really appreciate you getting the ticket."

Mom raised her hands and shook her head, smiling. "That was Doozy's idea."

"Well, I'll have to thank him," Luke said.

"Congratulations on the contest," Mom said. "Those bikes are really beautiful."

"Thank you so much. I'm excited about their production."

"I think several people turned in multiple designs, but you were the only one to draw a set. I loved the more delicate one of the same design. That was a great idea."

I came so close to mentioning that the girl bike was originally called the Ivy, but I didn't want to say that in front of my mom. Instead, I just smiled for apparently no reason.

"I appreciate it," Luke said graciously. "I was really thankful for the opportunity to have your family look at my work."

"Doozy's thrilled about it," she said. "He called me just a minute ago, asking if you were here yet."

Luke gestured with his palms up. "I'm here," he said.

I couldn't stop myself. I lunged in, grabbing him around the waist and resting my head on his chest. "He's here," I said. "Tell Doozy we'll ride by the shop in a little bit."

"He's not there," Mom said. "He's home."

She was regarding me like she was slightly surprised by the fact that I unashamedly latched onto Luke. I had never been like this with anybody, and I knew she was noticing it. She didn't say anything, though.

"Tell Doozy and Shug we'll go by their house, then," I said.

Mom nodded. "Any plans for tonight? I was gonna cook something easy, maybe tacos or spaghetti."

"We'll probably ride for a little while, and then go by Shug's. I want to take him by my house. We'll be at the house for some dinner, though."

Mom nodded and then looked at Luke. "Do you have a vote?" she asked. "Tacos or spaghetti?"

"Either of those sound great," he said.

155

She smiled and looked at him thoughtfully before reaching up to touch his cheek. "Take care of my daughter," she said.

She was poised to leave, and she made the statement sound like it was instructions for our immediate future (while I was on the back of a motorcycle with him). But I knew my mom, and she meant it for more than that. She could see that something deeper was transpiring between us.

"I promise I will take the best possible care of her." Luke squeezed my shoulders when he spoke to my mom. We all knew his promise wasn't just about the motorcycle ride, either.

Chapter 16

It had been a while since I had ridden on the back of the motorcycle. I rode all the time, but there was rarely a cause for me to hitch a ride with my dad or brothers. I honestly couldn't remember the last time I had been on the back of a bike.

I really didn't know what to expect with Luke. I knew he loved motorcycles, and I figured he would be a good driver, but I was amazed by the way he took over, treating my dad's bike like it was his own. He maintained complete control as he started the engine and held the bike steady for me to climb on.

Somewhere deep down, I was afraid that I would compare him to my family members and that he would come up lacking, but he knew what he was doing on a motorcycle. I held onto his waist, and we left the airport. He didn't know where I wanted to go, so I gave him directions as we went, stretching up to speak loudly next to his ear every time I wanted him to make a turn.

On our way to Shug and Doozy's, we went down a long, deserted road. It wasn't really on our way, but it also wasn't too far out of the way, so I took him over there. It was a road he and I had been down before, during his last visit, and I wanted to see if he remembered it.

"This isn't the way to your grandparents'," Luke said, turning to yell at me once he realized where we were.

"It's not too far out of the way," I said. "And I thought you might want to open it up a little."

It was a road the Bishops traveled all the time—especially to try out or break in a new bike. It was wide open, and there was never any traffic and no speed limit signs were posted. We affectionately called it 'the strip' because it was so straight and smooth.

Taking Luke to the strip wasn't a test, but if it would have been, he would have passed with flying colors. He rode like the wind. He was in total and complete control of the machine. I felt his body flex and bend as he counterbalanced. I held on tightly, relishing the feel of his taut stomach under my arms.

The bike was loud, and the low rumble of the engine only added to my breathlessness. Luke sped, but not so fast that it scared me. I didn't glance at the speedometer when he really opened it up, but I knew he pushed the limits right to the point where he could show me that he was in control without putting us in any danger. He operated the bike like someone who had been doing it his whole life. He rode like a Bishop.

Luke took me down the strip and back before making a right hand turn on Briarwood to go to Shug's. Apparently, he remembered how to get to their house now that I had brought him this far. I started to give him directions at every turn, but just before I spoke, I could feel him shift, and I knew he remembered where he was going.

Luke was still on the motorcycle when I got off of it at Shug's. We both had on helmets, and we took them off, simultaneously smiling at each other and running our hands through our hair.

"That was so fun," I said.

"I bet it was more fun for me."

I smiled and shook my head as I handed him my helmet. He hung them both from the handlebars. He was still sitting on the seat, and I walked over to stand right next to him—so close that my leg touched his. He was slightly shorter than me now that he was sitting down, and I stared down at him, feeling like I could get lost in his dark eyes.

"I thought I didn't like riding with someone else," I said. "But I was so wrong. That was the best ever."

He grinned and shook his head at me, and I got lost, staring at his mouth. I really loved the shape of it so much, and my stomach flipped at the memory of kissing it at the airport. I desperately wanted to do it again.

"What?" I said.

"What do you mean, what?"

"What are you shaking your head at?" I asked.

"I just can't believe it's you," he said. "I can't believe you're standing right here looking at me like this."

159

"Like what? Like I love you? Like I want to kiss you?"

"Yes, and yes," he said thoughtfully, lightly wrapping his hand around the back of my leg. He let it rest there.

"Well, I do, and I do," I said, staring at him seriously. I felt his hand move on the back of my leg, squeezing gently to pull me closer.

"Hey, y'all!" Shug yelled from the porch.

I turned to wave at her, and I felt Luke's hand leave my leg so fast that it was almost like he'd been burned. I had to smile.

"Hey, Shug!" I yelled.

I turned and watched as Luke got off the bike. He had zipped his jacket for the ride, and he unzipped it halfway as he stood and straightened. He was irresistibly handsome. I assumed, based on the speed at which he removed his hand from my leg, that he was reluctant to show too much affection in front of my family, but I could not stop myself from holding onto him. I wrapped my arm around his waist, snuggling into his side as we walked. I pulled him toward the house.

"Hey there, Luke!" Shug yelled.

"Hello, Mrs. Bishop," he yelled back.

My ear was right next to his body, and his deep voice reverberated in his chest, causing my breath to hitch. I smiled, feeling so very nostalgic. I loved every single thing about this man. Simply walking next to him comforted me.

Doozy joined Shug on the porch, and they both walked out, onto the pathway to greet us. "Looks like you took out Black Beauty," Doozy said, referring to my dad's bike and calling it by a nickname and not the actual model name. "How'd she handle?"

"Like a dream," Luke said. He let go of me long enough to reach out and shake Doozy's hand. "My whole day has been kinda like that."

"Like what?" Shug asked, leaning in to hug him.

"Like a dream," Luke said.

Shug smiled and sighed as she took him in. "You mean coming here to see Ivy?" she asked.

Luke glanced at me. "Yes, ma'am, I do," he said.

I reached up and put my hand on his face. "Isn't he so handsome?" I asked, talking to Shug but not taking my eyes off of him. He smiled shyly and shook his head at me.

"See what I mean?" he asked, referring to this day being a dream.

Shug shot me a look like Luke was the sweetest thing ever. She linked arms with him, and we all headed toward the house. They tried to feed us, but I told her Mom was cooking and that we had just come by for a visit.

We sat around the living room and talked for I don't know how long—hours. Shug and Doozy had a big house, but it was cozy and welcoming, and we all just found spots on couches. My grandparents sat on the big couch, and Luke and I took a smaller one.

161

I felt like sitting right on his lap—I felt like I couldn't possibly get close enough to him—but I settled for sitting next to him.

At first, we spoke about various topics, like music, and London, and my work with the kids at Memphis Learning Center, but once Doozy mentioned motorcycles, it was all over. It was really an eye-opening experience hearing Luke talk shop with Doozy. I was aware that Luke knew a lot about motorcycles, but the way he talked to my grandfather gave me a new appreciation for just how knowledgeable he was. Luke hadn't had too much one-on-one time with my grandfather during his first visit, so it was their first time to really relax and talk.

Doozy had met his match.

Luke was just as passionate about motorcycles as he was. They smiled and laughed the whole time, talking about various aspects of bikes and bike building that I didn't even know existed. They bounced ideas and experiences off of each other in a way that made me proud of Luke. I had never seen Doozy take to somebody the way he took to him. In spite of their age difference, they were like long-lost best friends. It gave me the strangest sense of happiness and fulfillment to see them having so much fun together.

"Luke, I'd like to like to offer you a promotion if you're up for it," Doozy said.

This comment came after a long talk. I had been zoning out, thinking about something else just before he said it, but my ears perked up when I heard the word *promotion*.

"I'd be honored," Luke said. "I don't even know what you have in mind, but I'm up for it, whatever it is."

This statement pleased Doozy. He smiled and shifted in his seat, propping his ankle on his knee. "I'd like you to start designing for us. You wouldn't make commission like you're doing with the contest bike. That was a one-time thing. You would be on straight salary. We don't need to discuss exact terms right this second, and you don't need to give me an answer, but it's something to think about. I don't know what you're making now, but I'm sure it'd be a nice little bump. I'd be honored to have you, and we'd treat you well. It'd be a good living."

"Michael doesn't go around offering promotions to people," Shug said, looking impressed.

Doozy laughed. "I'm just being smart. If I don't treat this boy well, he's gonna find somebody who will. Shoot, he'd do it on his own if he had to. Lord knows, I don't want to find myself competing with the Wright Motorcycle Company in few years."

We all laughed. "I love your company, Mr. Bishop," Luke said. "It'd really be an honor to design for you."

I was praying this meant he'd have no other choice but to move to Memphis, but Doozy's next words left me feeling a little deflated.

"I know you live in London, but that's okay; you can do it from anywhere. We'll talk more about it. I'll probably still have you working at the dealership; we'll just give you an office and a new set of responsibilities. If you're anything like me, which I know you are, you'll want to still get your hands dirty. We'll work it out where you can do that if you decide to take the offer."

"I want it," Luke said. "I'll take it. Whatever you're offering, I want it."

Doozy smiled and scooted to the edge of the couch so that he could lean over and shake Luke's hand. "Congratulations, then, son. Consider yourself promoted."

Luke shook his hand. "Thank you very much," he said with a smile. "I'm excited."

"This is cause for celebration," Shug said. "I wish y'all could stay for dinner."

"Mom's already cooking," I said. "But I'm sure y'all can come over there."

"Liam and Taylor are going out to eat," Shug said. "They're bringing little Mack over here in a few minutes so Doozy and I can spoil him."

I sighed as I stood up. "We should be going," I said. I turned to glance at Luke, but he was already in the process of standing up. "Tell Liam and Taylor 'hey' for me." I said.

"I will," Shug said.

She and Doozy both got up to walk us to the door. They hugged us and thanked us for coming by.

Luke and Doozy had another exchange about the promotion, and again, my grandfather mentioned that he was excited about giving Luke more responsibility.

We had stayed at Shug and Doozy's for so long that rather than stop by my new house, we went straight to my parents'. I had received a text from my mom saying that dinner was ready, so I figured we'd eat and then I'd show him my place afterward.

I marveled at how much I loved riding on a motorcycle with him. The trip to my parents' house was short, and I found myself wishing it had taken us a lot longer to get there. I told him to pull the bike into the garage, and he did, parking it next to mine.

He killed the engine, and we got off of the motorcycle, standing next to each other. I peered up at him, feeling like I had never in my life been so smitten. His mouth wasn't just gorgeous looking. Out of it came intelligent, heartfelt words, and I found that I loved him more and more with every passing moment.

"You got a new job just now," I said, stepping closer to him. I held both of his hands, and we stood there, letting our clasped hands absentmindedly rise as we both bent our elbows. He took a deep breath, regarding me thoughtfully.

"I, uh, I haven't really had any sleep since you called me at the pub, and I, uh…"

"I'm sorry," I said. "You must be exhausted, and I'm running you all around town, making you drive me around and visit with my family."

I led our hands downward, but I kept them clasped with his, stepping even closer to him.

"Ivy, I'm not saying that so you'll apologize. I'm just saying... the job... and talking to your grandfather... and you... it's all so... I honestly feel like I'm dreaming. I have the feeling I'm gonna wake up in my own flat, and this will all have been just a—"

I stopped him by repositioning a little. I gently wrapped my arms around his waist. "You're not dreaming," I whispered. "You're here. In America. With me."

He cupped his hands around my cheeks. "Say it again," he said softly.

"You're not dreaming," I said. "You're here. Right here in my arms. You're about to eat my mom's tacos, and then we're gonna go down the street so you can see my house." I really almost said "our house", but I managed to stop myself.

"And the job?" he asked.

"Doozy basically begged you to take it," I said. "He loves you. I can't believe how much he loves you."

Luke nodded. "Okay, so, I'm not gonna wake up in London?"

I shook my head, smiling at him. "Nope."

Chapter 17

Owen and Darcy came over to eat tacos with us. They brought the twins, of course, and their dog, Henry, who loved to roam around in my parents' backyard. Daniel and Courtney would have come as well, but she had an event going on at the art center, and she ended up taking the whole family.

Owen was a protective older brother, and he could see how much I liked Luke, so he had question after question for him. He was also my only brother who had worked at the family business his whole life, so eventually, his personal questions turned to motorcycle talk. Just as he did with Doozy, Luke won Owen over with his knowledge, love, and passion for motorcycles. Before I knew it, Owen and Dad were both asking Luke questions that I didn't even understand about fabricating parts and various tools.

Sometime during all that motorcycle talk, Owen brought up the subject of knife throwing. Luke asked if any of us had been practicing, and we all admitted that we weren't nearly as disciplined about it as we once had been. I told him I had gotten pretty decent at it for a while, but I had been so busy with work during the past six-months or so that I had scarcely even picked up a knife. Dad said he went out to the target and threw "every once in a while".

Then, Mom asked Luke if he still practiced, and his answer surprised me.

"Yes ma'am, I kind of have to. Jolene roped me into posting on her YouTube channel while she's traveling with Wes."

My head whipped around to stare at Luke when he said that. I had no idea.

My mom appeared to be as surprised as I was. "Oh, so you've been making videos?" she asked.

Luke nodded. "Jo didn't want her channel to be idle while she's traveling, so she asked me to post for her. My mom helps me with the filming and editing and everything. I don't know much about that stuff, and honestly, I don't really have the desire to learn. I just practice enough knife throwing to make her subscribers think I know what I'm talking about. I have to think of about five-minutes of material to post once a week. My mom does the rest. She bought a fancy computer, and she's gotten pretty good at it." He shrugged. "Jolene's not picky as long as something's getting posted."

"So, you've been practicing," I said. "Basically, you've gotten a lot better while all of us have been slacking off."

Luke laughed. "I don't know if I have gotten a lot better, but yes, I have been practicing."

"I guess we need to go outside and see the fruits of your labor," Owen said.

I looked at him sideways, wondering if he was challenging Luke, and he just smiled at me. "I'm

168

going out there, anyway," he said. "We have to be getting home, and I need to check on Henry and make sure he didn't get too muddy to ride in the Tahoe."

"I'll throw some with y'all, if you want to," Dad said.

Before I knew what was happening, everyone was going outside. I had to use the restroom, so I promised I'd meet them out there in a minute.

It's funny how much internet research you can do in two minutes, from your phone, in the restroom. I went to YouTube, found Jolene's channel, and clicked on the most recent video "she" had posted.

There he was, in all his handsome glory.

I pressed play and then almost panicked when the video began playing and I realized my phone was turned all the way up. His voice came over the speaker loudly, and I quickly muted it, looking around to make sure I hadn't been caught even though I was in the bathroom by myself.

I turned it up just loud enough to hear what he was saying, and I concentrated on the screen. He was confident and matter of fact as he told about the technique he was practicing in the video. It was something about proper thumb grip. I knew I didn't have much time, so I only watched the first thirty seconds or so, but it was enough to give me that achy feeling in my gut. I desired him more than I had ever desired anyone. I wanted him to just come out and say that he would be mine—that he would always be mine, always and forever.

I couldn't just sit there and watch the rest of the video, though. That would be crazy when I could go out there and see him throw knives in person. Before I closed the browser, I used my thumb to scroll down. The video was posted four days ago, and it already had over a hundred thousand views.

How does a knife throwing video get so many views? And one about proper thumb grip at that.

There were eight thousand comments.

What in the world?

I had to look.

The first few were vague things like "Thanks," or "Nice video." A few of them were long with lots of knife throwing jargon, and I just scanned them without really reading. After scrolling past what must have been ten or fifteen or so comments, I got to one that said, "You're hot," and then another that said, "Bae," and then even further, I saw, "Marry me, pleeeeease!!!!"

Those lovey-dovey, infatuated feelings I was experiencing quickly turned to some crazy odd mixture of jealousy and pride. I knew girls had been crazy about Derek, but I had never been this jealous over him.

I had only looked at the first page of comments. *What in the world would I have seen if I had looked at all eight-thousand of them? Why were so many girls subscribed to Jolene's channel, anyway?*

170

There was no time to care.

I turned off my phone and slipped it into my pocket.

"Did you throw yet?" I asked when I stepped outside. Everyone was standing around, but I was looking at Luke when I said it, so he was the one who answered.

He shook his head, and I went to stand next to him. After watching that video, I felt like I wanted to claim him in some way—announce to my family in some grand proclamation that we were officially together. I settled for standing next to him. I stood close enough to bump his arm with my shoulder, and he looked at me with a smile.

Owen had taken a turn at the target, and he came over to Luke, holding the knives out for him. Luke took them from my brother, but he promptly offered them to me. He didn't say anything, he just looked at me with his eyebrows raised as if to ask if I wanted them.

I shook my head, and he took that as his queue. He went to stand at the ten-foot line and squared up with the target, taking a deep breath.

Darcy had Cole on her hip, and my dad was holding Colin. Luke glanced at Henry who was sitting on his haunches next to Darcy. He proceeded to do something I'd never seen. He threw all ten knives, one after the other. He didn't go for speed or showmanship. He was calm and collected, aiming carefully before he let each of them fly through the air.

I didn't realize what he was doing until he was almost finished. It was a heart. He threw the ten knives, and the final result was ten knives sticking out of the target in the obvious shape of a heart.

It was the most magical thing I had ever seen. I was stunned.

"Is that a heart?" Darcy asked in an amazed tone.

"Oh, my goodness, it is!" Mom said, stepping forward to get a closer look at the target. "That's amazing! How'd you learn to do that?"

Luke smiled and shook his head. "You can thank my sister," he said. "I told her if she wanted help with her channel she had to give me ideas, and she came up with that one for Valentine's Day."

"I bet you could do any shape, though," Mom said.

Luke nodded as he went to pull the knives from the board. "Yes ma'am. I just have more practice at a heart."

He joined us on the side, holding out the knives for me.

I shook my head. "I'm not following that," I said, smiling at him.

"Me neither," Dad said.

"Don't look at me," Darcy added.

"We need to go anyway," Owen said. "That was awesome, though." He glanced at our mom. "Thanks for dinner."

"We need to go, too," I said. "I want to bring Luke to the house before it's too dark to see anything."

We could have walked to my house, but we took my car instead. It would have taken ten minutes for us to get there had we walked, and we were quickly losing sunlight. The exterior was almost completely done, except for some finishing touches. The painters had been there a week before, and after the Hardie Board got some color, it really started to feel like home.

"Oh, Ivy, it's amazing!" Luke said, as we pulled into the driveway. "I can't believe this is yours!"

"Thank you. I love it. I can't believe it either. When it's not so dark out, you can see the blue better."

"I can see it just fine," he said, getting out of the car.

I grabbed his hand on the way inside. "Do you like it?" I asked, holding onto his arm.

He shifted to look down at me. "Are you kidding? I love it. It's so beautiful. I love the property, too. I can't believe you have woods."

"What about the blue?" I asked. "Do you think it's a good shade?"

"It's perfect. You did so good."

We slowly made our way onto the porch and through the front door. Luke looked at all the details, mentioning things he liked as we meandered. He asked a ton of questions—big, obvious things like how many bedrooms and how many square feet, and little things like whether my stove was gas or electric and what kind of knobs I was going to put on the doors. I showed him some of my favorite features, and I loved how enthusiastic he was about everything.

It had gotten pretty dark in the house as I showed him around. I had a couple of lanterns, but rather than continue walking around in the dark, I pulled him onto the back porch. It was one of my absolute favorite places. I had always loved porches, so I built a big one. I adored being outside and I had always been drawn to porch swings. Plus, with the way my house was situated, my back porch had a beautiful view of the sunset.

"You're kidding," he said in amazement, looking around when I led him out the back door. "This is really something."

The porch was ten feet deep and thirty feet long. It was completely covered and had a wood rail, making it feel altogether cozy and wonderful. I knew I would spend a ton of time out there. I had a clearing for a backyard with a view of the woods that lined the other side. We could hear the sounds of nature as we stood there.

"There's a fox," I said.

"Where?"

"He's not out there right now, but I do have one. The construction crew leaves their leftovers out by the tree line, and he comes to eat. He's huge. He's got a big ol' bushy tail."

"You've seen him?" Luke asked.

I nodded. I reached out for his hand, pulling him to the right side of the porch where I would eventually hang a swing. There were a few chairs sitting around, one of which was an extremely comfortable, heavy duty rocking chair. My mom had four or five of them, and she had Dad bring one over so I could begin to enjoy my porch.

I led Luke to it, and without saying a word, got the point across to him that I wanted him to have a seat in it. He sat down, and I proceeded to sit on his lap, favoring one side, and letting my legs hang between his. He smiled and held onto me, adjusting his seating position so that we could both get comfortable. I leaned against his chest, falling into his embrace.

"What do you think?" I asked. "Do you like it?"

He rocked several times without saying a thing. He just sat there, holding onto me. I knew he had heard my question, so I didn't ask it again. I simply sat there and waited for him to answer.

"Ivy, 'yes' isn't an adequate word. I started to say *I love it*, but that doesn't feel good enough, either. You've got a little piece of heaven here. I'm so happy for you, I really am. I can't believe this is yours."

My head was resting in the crook of his neck, but I shifted so that I could stare at him. Our faces were only a few inches apart, and he continued to stare out at the view.

"I wish you would share it with me," I said.

This caused him to look at me.

"I know you love me," I said.

His gorgeous smile broadened. "How do you know?"

"Because, I just do. You named your motorcycle after me. You called it the Ivy. Doozy told me."

"He did?"

I nodded.

"What if that was for your grandma?"

I squinted at him, and he smiled.

"I saw your YouTube video," I said. "I watched a few seconds of one. I searched it when I went to the bathroom at Mom's."

"Oh yeah? What'd you think?"

"That you're the most handsome man I've ever seen and that I wanted the whole world to know you're mine."

"All that from a video?" he asked.

"Just a little *piece* of a video," I said.

Luke shifted, faking like he was reaching for his pocket. "I've got my phone right here," he said, groaning as if he was actually trying for it, which he wasn't. "We should definitely watch some more."

I laughed, relishing the feel of his body shifting as I leaned against him. "I don't need to watch any more." I said. "I'm already ate up with it."

"With what?" he asked, relaxing again.

"Smittenness."

I rested my head on his chest, unashamedly curling up into his arms and snuggling against him. I expected him to say something about my variation of the word smitten, but he didn't. He just held me, gently rocking in the chair.

It was cool but not cold and the evening sun was peeking out from behind the trees. I breathed deeply. I couldn't imagine a more perfect moment.

Chapter 18

Luke and I sat in that rocking chair, watching the sun disappear. I stared at the glowing orange ball moving downward behind the trees, and it went from dusk to night right before my eyes. For what must have been at least ten minutes, we sat there in comfortable silence, listening to the sounds of nature—the wind, and the frogs and crickets.

"Luke?" I whispered.

"Huh?" the sound came from his chest, and he delivered it quickly as if he was somewhat surprised.

"Were you sleeping?" I asked.

"I don't think so," he said. "Just closing my eyes." His voice was even lower than usual, telling me that if he hadn't been sleeping, he was, at least, really tired. I sat up just enough to look at him.

"You wanna head back to the house?" I asked.

He shook his head slowly.

"No? Why not?"

"Because I'm too comfortable. If we go back, that means I have to let you go."

I wriggled just a little with sheer pleasure, and that made him chuckle, causing his chest to shake. I stretched upward, placing a tender kiss on his neck, and then one further up, on his cheek.

"Ivy."

"What?" I whispered close to his ear.

"Your family, their business, this legacy."

"What about it?"

"I knew it was something special. It was special to me before I even knew you." He spoke slowly and deliberately, and I relaxed in his arms, feeling comforted by his voice. "Jolene fell in love with Wes, and I got to come here and meet your family. It was all just so surreal. It was better to me than meeting the queen or the president. Seriously, if I had the choice of meeting those people or meeting your family, I would definitely have chosen your family. I had this idea of you before we even met, before I even knew you. In my mind, you were royalty. Jolene was marrying into royalty. Even if you weren't so beautiful, you still would have been the heir to the Bishop name—you still would have had this awesome, magical place in my mind. I would have still wanted to impress you just based on your name alone."

He paused, but I just sat in his lap, not knowing where he was going with all this.

"But then I saw you, Ivy. I saw you with my own eyes, and you were so beautiful—really and truly the most precious thing I had ever seen—even more beautiful than your pictures. And I talked to you, and found out that you were funny, and kind, and compassionate, and determined, and somehow innocent yet really smart at the same time. You turned out to be this amazing jewel, this amazing prize, and it had nothing to do with your family. You were wonderful on your own—you were brilliant without your name. I would have fallen in love with you even if you weren't a Bishop. You are altogether lovely, Ivy, and it has nothing to do with your family." He took a deep breath. "And then, I remember that you're a Bishop, and that's what makes me feel like this whole thing is a dream. It truly feels like it can't be real. I'm holding you in my arms, and I still can't help but doubt it. I haven't done anything to deserve this, yet here I am."

I kissed him again. I let my mouth fall gently onto his cheek and I held it there, letting it linger. I tasted his skin—felt the texture of his smooth cheek under my lips. I moved to speak near his ear.

"I don't feel like I deserve you, either, Luke. I remembered the picture of you with that girl, the redhead—the one you showed me when you first came here. I thought you would still be with her. I called you thinking I was gonna have to do something desperate and try to break up some happy relationship. I called, and you answered, and you weren't with her anymore. I didn't even have to get desperate and break y'all up. And now here you are—throwing knives into heart shapes and impressing my family with all your amazingness. You're the handsome prince who wrote me the magical letter, and you dropped everything and left London to come to me."

I paused, but he didn't say anything right away, so I continued.

"I saw some comments on that video you posted, talking about you and how good-looking you were, and I felt like I wanted to ring those girls' necks. I'm jealous over you, Luke. Dreadfully jealous. I remembered that time we spent together last time you were here, and I realized I fell in love with you even back then. And then, you come here, and I see you talking to Doozy and to my dad and Owen about motorcycles. I see how you fit in with this family and how they respect you and want you to be a part of what they're doing—not just because I want them to, but because they truly admire you. I see all that, and I feel like *I'm* the one who's dreaming, Luke. I wonder how I ended up here, on my porch, sitting on your lap. I'm afraid to go to sleep, too. I'm afraid I'll wake up and this will all have been a dream."

"Maybe neither of us are dreaming, then," he said.

I sighed. "Maybe not."

I was still resting on his shoulder, but I could see the side of his face. I stared at his mouth—the way his top lip protruded out past the bottom one. The looks of it caused sensations in my gut—warm, desirous sensations. I wanted him to kiss me so badly that I ached with it. I sat up, turning and positioning myself in front of him.

He grinned at me, and reached out to touch the side of my face. His fingers laced through my hair, and his thumb grazed my temple. I wanted my mouth on him so badly, that I turned my face toward his palm, letting my lips fall onto the base of his hand. My mouth was opened slightly and I gently pulled the skin of his hand into my mouth, kissing it, tasting it. I heard Luke let out a labored breath, which pleased me greatly.

"Ivy," he said.

I left my mouth on his hand, but I glanced at him out of the corner of my eye. He wrapped his hand around the back of my head, using it to pull my face closer to his. I knew what he was going to do, and I wanted it more than I have never wanted anything in my life.

I absolutely yearned to kiss him.

Finally, he did it. He pressed his lips to mine, and the relief we both felt was palpable.

What followed was no airport kiss.

It began gently with a few delicate kisses where I let my mouth wrap around his glorious upper lip. It felt and tasted just like I thought it would. Luke gently sucked my lower lip into his mouth, and the wet warmth of it caused me to crumple in his arms. I was all his—desperately melting into his arms, full of warm desire.

I opened my mouth to him, and he held me tightly and kissed me deeply. He didn't stop, either. We kissed for a long time. We kissed like it was our very first time to kiss anyone—like we were just figuring out what kissing was about and how fun it could be. Several times, we readjusted in the chair, moving this way and that and getting comfortable before going right on kissing some more.

We kissed so gently at times that our mouths barely brushed. We kissed so passionately at times that we squeezed each other tightly and our teeth bumped.

I got to know Luke in a different way during that kiss—I got to know and appreciate his divine, full mouth in a way that I couldn't do with my eyes. This kiss showed me things I didn't know before. It made me realize that I desired him like a wife desires a husband.

I wanted Luke's to be the only lips I kissed for the rest of my life, and I wanted him to kiss no one else but me. I suspected it before, but this kiss made me know it—he was the one. He was mine and I was his, and I just wouldn't settle for anything less.

We sat on my porch for—

Honestly, I had no idea how long we sat there.

I think it might have been hours.

My mouth was wonderfully swollen and sensitive by the time I sat back, took a deep breath, and came to my senses.

"What time is it?" I asked. Luke leaned to the side, pulling his phone out of his back pocket.

We both looked at it as he pressed the home button. It was after 9pm, and the realization of how late it was caused me to glance at him.

"Wow," I said in a matter of fact tone. "Time flies." I didn't have to add the bit about *when you're having fun*, because Luke knew what I meant.

"Yep, it does," he agreed.

"Do you want to get married?" I asked, still matter of fact.

He grinned, thinking I was messing around.

"I'm serious," I said. "Not right this second or anything, but soon. Do you want to marry me?" I glanced around. "You could just move in here with me, if you want."

"You sound like you're being serious," he said.

"I am being serious."

"You're probably just a little delirious," he said.

I shook my head, feeling slightly heartbroken. I thought he would just agree the instant I suggested it. I tried to hide it, but I think I made a disappointed expression. "You're the one who's delirious, not me," I said.

"Then, I'm probably hearing you wrong."

"You're breaking my heart," I said. "I thought you felt the same as me, and I—"

Luke stopped me by putting his hands on the sides of my face. He held me steady as he stared into my eyes with a serious expression. "I love you, Ivy Bishop. I have never loved anything as much as I love you. I never even knew it was possible to love anything this much."

"But what?" I asked.

"But your dad and brothers would kill me if I tried to come over here and marry you like this. They're protective of you. They're gonna think it's too fast."

"Why do you care what they think?"

He shrugged. "I don't, but *you* do. You're gonna ask me to marry you, and I'm gonna take you seriously, and then your family's gonna remind you that it's a crazy idea, and I'm gonna end up all heartbroken and dissapoin—"

He stopped talking during mid-sentence, and smiled at me because I made a big scowl, scrunching up my face at him—wrinkling my nose and everything. I held the expression long enough to cause him to laugh. His chest shook as he stared at me.

"I honestly don't care what they think, Luke. I mean that with all sincerity. I know I want to marry you. I really do. I got to know you as a person at a time when I couldn't follow my attraction, and then, for a year, I lived with that letter you wrote—those words that were from your heart to my heart. I just know it was meant to be like this. Me and you. I'm glad Wes found Jolene and they're happy and everything, but as far as I'm concerned, they were just a little bonus, a side project in the bigger plan. The real plan—the one to get you to me."

Luke still had my face in his hands, and as he regarded me, his smile turned to something else, something more earnest.

"Yes, then," he said. "Obviously, yes. I would love nothing more than to marry you, Ivy Bishop. You name a time and place, and I'm there."

I smiled. "That's better," I said.

Luke kissed me one last time while he still had his hands on my face, and then he took them away, giving my legs a little pat like he assumed we were about to stand up.

"You ready?" I asked.

He nodded and smiled at me with a long blink.

I knew he was running on empty. It had been far too long since he had any real sleep. I got up, stretching, and he stood beside me, doing the same thing. He reached out for me, taking me into his arms now that we were on our feet. I marveled at how tall and broad he was. I felt utterly safe and secure, like this man could protect me from anything.

Chapter 19

For the next five days, I did my best to ignore the fact that Luke would eventually have to go back to London. We spent all of our free time together, and I truly dreaded the time when he would have to leave. I knew it would come way sooner than I wanted it to, so I chose to think about it as little as possible. He would only be in Memphis for three more days before he had to go back.

He had customers and co-workers depending on him at the dealership. He had commitments that he needed to get back to over there. Luke was the steady, dependable type, and he didn't feel right about leaving his job or his parents under such hasty circumstances. He had friends and an apartment in London. He simply had things he needed to do. I understood that, because I had commitments in Memphis.

I hated the idea of being separated from him, though, and I really thought about going to London with him when he left. But the nonprofit was still in the development stages, and as the founder, I just couldn't leave for an extended amount of time.

The plan was that he would go back for three months. And then, in June, once the house was ready, he would come back to Memphis—this time for good.

Of course, there would also be a wedding, but nobody knew that yet. Luke and I kept the whole plan to ourselves, at least for the moment. We would tell them all before he left, but we didn't want to share it just yet. After all, Jolene didn't even know we were seeing each other. She had been on the road with my brother and had no idea that Luke came to Memphis. I made a family announcement asking anyone who talked to her not to tell her that he was here so that we could surprise her when she came back.

I remembered calling her that night when they were in Chicago. I had asked her for Luke's contact information but that was as much as she knew. So much had changed since then, and Jolene had no idea.

She and Wes had rolled into town last night, but we still hadn't seen them. I knew if I rushed them into coming over she would know something was up. They were supposed to come by at 10am this morning, and I was so excited about it that I could hardly sleep.

Luke and I had fallen asleep on the couch the night before, and he woke me up at 2am to tuck me into my bed. I was so amped about seeing Wes and Jolene and telling them the news, that I was up and down until 6:30 when I finally got out of bed and took a shower. I was dressed and ready for the day before 8am.

Luke had gotten showered and dressed by the time I finished, and he was waiting in the kitchen for me when I came out. I was dressed for work in my "teacher clothes", and Luke was looking sharp wearing jeans and a plaid button-down shirt. He would spend his day at the shop, but he would change once he got there if he felt like he would be doing something that would get his clothes dirty.

We spent the morning hours together since we had some time to kill before Wes and Jolene came over. We drank coffee, ate breakfast, talked, laughed, and speculated about how his sister would react to him being there.

It was a good thing I didn't apply lipstick when I was getting ready.

His lips were like magnets to mine.

I kissed him any chance I got.

It was 10am when I got a call from Wes saying they couldn't make it.

"We got a late start this morning," he said, sounding apologetic. "I know you have to get to work. We'll come by this afternoon."

"This afternoon?" I said, feeling disappointed. "Shoot, I was missing y'all."

"Mom said something about cooking tonight," Wes said. "We'll just plan on seeing you then."

I knew that would have to be okay. I knew if I pushed for anything else, Wes would know I was hiding something. "Okay, that sounds good," I said. "I'll see y'all then."

I hung up with my brother and made a sad face at Luke.

"What?" he asked, seeing my expression.

"They can't come right now," I said. "They must be tired from the trip. He said he'd see me tonight."

Luke shrugged. "It might be fun to surprise her with everybody here."

"You're right," I said. "I'll have to think of some way we can do it—we'll have to trick her somehow since my brothers will be here. Maybe we could make her think you're one of them." I stared into space, thinking of different ways we could surprise Jolene—games we could play, or things we could do to really get her good. I had always loved surprises, and I knew she was going to flip out when she realized her brother was in Memphis. "I'll think about it while I'm at work," I said. "There's got to be a way to blindfold her or something."

Luke laughed and shook his head at me for my shenanigans.

"Just make sure none of the guys at the shop mention anything," I said. "I hope they don't go up there today."

Luke gave me a reassuring smile. "I'm sure they won't," he said.

Within minutes, we left the house, Luke heading to the shop, and me heading to work.

I didn't get off work until 6pm.

I was hoping to leave earlier, but a perspective student came in right at 5, and I couldn't bring myself to rush.

I was nervous about Jolene finding out Luke was there, so I had been in touch with my family all afternoon. Mom said Jo and Wes had been home all day, recovering from their travels, and that she told them she would have dinner ready at 6:30.

This was pushing it for me. I really wanted to be there for the surprise, but the later it got, the more I felt like it wasn't going to be possible. None of us ever really listened to Mom when she said what time she would serve dinner—we all just came to the house whenever we could. I knew the whole family would probably beat me there even though I would arrive before 6:30.

I called Luke on my way to the house, and he picked up on the second ring.

"Hey," he said.

"Hey. Is she there yet?"

"Jolene? No."

I glanced at the clock on the dashboard of my car, which read 6:09. "Really?" I said. "She's not?"

I was genuinely surprised that she and Wes hadn't gotten there yet. I thought for sure I would have missed everything.

"I think I heard your mom talking to Wes on the phone," he said. "But they're not here yet."

I sighed. "I had to stay for a new student, but I'm on my way. I'll be there in like ten minutes at the latest."

"It's all good," he said. "They're not here yet."

"Are other people there?" I could hear commotion in the background, so I knew the answer to my question. What I should've asked was *who's all there*.

"Daniel, Owen, your aunt and her kids... I think almost everybody who's coming, but not Wes and Jolene."

"If they get there, can you please go hide in the back room so they won't see you?"

He let out a little laugh on the other end. He knew how very much I wanted to be there for the surprise. The fact that I wanted him to hide was something we had gone over at least five times.

"I promise I'll hide if they get here before you," he said, reassuring me.

"Thank you, I love you."

"I love you too," he said. "I'll see you in a minute."

We said goodbye and hung up the phone. I was so excited and nervous that I was shaking. I turned on a classic rock station. They were playing Led Zeppelin's *D'yer Mak'er*, and I adjusted the volume accordingly, singing along (with the lyrics I knew) at the top of my lungs.

I wouldn't say I sped, but I certainly didn't take my time getting to the house. I pulled up at 6:22, scanning the row of cars in the driveway, and feeling so relieved when I realized that neither Wes's nor Jolene's were among them.

The house was packed with people when I walked in. They were all standing and sitting around in the kitchen and living room. Everyone yelled at me when I walked in. The toddlers ran over to give me hugs, followed by a few of the adults. I yelled, "Hello, y'all," to everyone who was looking at me from across the room, and I greeted the munchkins before standing to embrace Shug, Aunt Jane, and Courtney who were standing near the place where I had walked in.

My mom was busy in the kitchen, and she made a kissyface at me while she checked on whatever was in the pot.

"Smells like spaghetti," I said.

"Close," she said. "I've got stuffed shells in the oven. She gestured at the pot. "This is broccoli."

Stuffed shells were my favorite, and she knew it. I smiled thankfully at her, and she winked at me.

Luke was standing at the edge of the kitchen, but he waited for me to pass out hugs to everyone who was standing near the door. Once I greeted them and set down my things, I walked over to him. He was wearing the same jeans and plaid shirt that I had seen him in that morning, but his handsomeness still somehow took me by surprise. He smiled, and it caused a tingling sensation in my lower abdomen.

I walked directly into his arms, feeling so thankful that he seemed as relieved to see me as I was to see him. I squeezed him, breathing in the clean, familiar, masculine smell before stretching up to give him a kiss. I had to get on my tiptoes, and even then, he had to lean down for our lips to connect. I vaguely knew we were being watched, but I didn't care. In fact, I wanted everyone to see.

"They're here!" Shelby's voice came from the living room, and I turned to find her standing next to the window.

I craned my neck to glance out of the dining room window, and, indeed, I saw Wes's truck headed up the driveway.

I looked up at Luke. "That was close!" I said.

He lifted his eyebrows and nodded at me.

My eyes widened as I regarded him. "You have to hide!" I said. I let him go, stepping back. "Okay, y'all just play it cool!" I announced loudly enough for everyone to hear. "Nobody mention somebody being here. I've got a way to surprise her. Y'all just keep doing what you're doing and don't look suspicious. Just play along with what I say."

I tried to make my warning speech as kid-friendly as possible. I knew if I said they specifically shouldn't mention *Luke*, that would be the first thing out of their mouths. Luke walked down the hall, and everyone else went about their business, looking as inconspicuous as possible.

Within a minute, Wes and Jolene came to the door, and we all yelled at them and greeted them the same way everyone had done for me. It had been a while since any of us had seen them, so there was a little extra excitement surrounding their arrival. Basically, everyone who was in the kitchen made their way to the entryway to greet them. My mom even put down her spoon so that she could go to the door and see them.

Wes was in the middle of tickling little Cora when Kip walked up to Jolene. He tugged at her pants.

"Why awe we not suppose to look se-pi-shus?"

"Why what?" she asked, smiling and glancing at Courtney for translation.

"He's into dinosaurs lately," Courtney said dismissively. "Go get your T-rex so you can show Wes and JoJo."

Kip ran off, and Courtney turned to give me a wide-eyed glance at how close that had been.

I had a plan about how to surprise Jolene. I had already talked to my mom about it, but I knew I couldn't rush it, so I just walked up and greeted like everyone else, trying to act as natural as possible.

"Did you get in touch with my brother?" she asked casually.

"Oh, that, no. I mean, I-I think I ended up just emailing him."

It was a ridiculous lie, but I was so nervous that it just came out. She hadn't even given me his email address. *What was I thinking?* Fortunately, Jolene didn't seem to think twice about it. There were so many people standing around who had questions for her and Wes that she easily went on to other things.

"Dinner's gonna be a few more minutes," Mom announced a moment later once everybody had the chance to settle down. "I think Ivy's got a game for y'all to play while we're waiting."

Chapter 20

It was not out of the ordinary for me to make everyone participate in some sort of game or contest, so no one thought it suspicious that I wanted to play a game while we waited for dinner. Everyone besides Wes and Jolene knew what was going on, anyway, and they played along, gathering around the big kitchen peninsula.

My mom already had pencils and paper handy for the big moment. She even had a scarf for blindfolding, which was super prepared of her.

"Okay, so some of y'all will remember this one," I said, getting everyone's attention as I absentmindedly shifted the papers. "It's one we used to play a long time ago."

There were a ton of people at the house, so a few of them lost interest, talking amongst themselves in the back of the group or tending to the children. All of them were gathered around, though, which was only happening because everyone wanted to see the surprise. (Usually, I could only rope about five or six at a time into playing my games.)

"So, it's like Pictionary, only the person drawing has no idea what they're doing. They just follow the instructions that are given to them."

"Oh, I remember this," Wes said.

I nodded at him. "So, let's say the word is television." I said. "The person drawing the TV has no idea what they're drawing. They put on the blindfold and follow the instructions given to them. Only one person knows the clue, and they're trying to make us all guess it by telling the blindfolded person what to draw. Does that make sense?" Before anyone could answer I said, "Look, it's easy. Let's just play, and you'll see. Wes, you can start. You can give the clues to Jolene."

Jolene looked a little reluctant to be the first one chosen to play, but I thrust the blindfold into her hands, not giving her a choice.

"Okay, sit right here," I said.

I positioned her on a stool with the paper right in front of her. Behind her back, I shot a conspiratorial look to my mother. She knew to go and get Luke from the back room, and she smiled and nodded at me.

"Okay, Jo, so you just do what Wes tells you, and we will all try to guess what you're drawing."

"So, *he* knows what I'm drawing but I don't?" Jolene clarified.

I nodded. "I'm going to tell Wes an object, and he has to give you instructions like, draw two small squares on top of each other, and things like that. He'll say *'on the right or left'*, and *'higher or lower'*, and give you instructions like that."

Jolene looked a little hesitant. "Are you sure we shouldn't let someone try it who knows what they're doing?"

"No, no, no, you'll be fine. You're an artist. It's easy, you'll see."

She made a silly fearful face as she put on the blindfold.

"Can you see anything?" I asked.

"No."

I could see my mother pulling Luke out of the hallway, and I watched, feeling delirious with nerves and adrenaline as they silently but quickly crossed the living room, headed toward us. Wes was standing right next to me, and I squeezed his arm tightly enough to cause him to look at me. I put my finger to my lips and made a face, pleading with him to keep quiet about Luke's arrival. I began winking—that over exaggerated wink that let Wes know that whatever I was about to say was a lie.

"Okay, let me tell Wes the object," I said, talking to Jolene. "He's going to give you the clues in just a second. Are you sure you can't see?"

She touched the blindfold. "I'm sure," she said.

I kept my eyes trained on Wes, begging him not to say anything as I pulled Luke toward me. I was about to whisper into Luke's ear, but I was afraid I would say it too loud, so I grabbed a piece of paper, and wrote down the word "snowman". I was so anxious that I nearly flashed it for the whole crowd to see. It wouldn't have mattered, anyway, since we weren't really playing the game.

"Got it?" I asked.

Luke nodded.

"Okay, you guys have two minutes. If you can't make them guess it in two minutes, we'll let somebody else go."

"I'm nervous!" Jolene said, taking the words out of my mouth. "Are my hands in the right place?"

I glanced at her right hand, which was holding a pencil and positioned right in the middle of the paper. "Yes," I said. "Perfect."

The kids were in the living room. My dad was keeping them preoccupied while the whole thing went down. I nervously shifted my gaze around the bar. Everybody was smiling and watching us to see what would happen.

I gave the word… "On your mark, get set, go!"

"Okay," Luke said. "Draw, three circles on top of each other, and make the bottom one the biggest."

Yikes. It was too good of a first clue, and I cringed, fearing that someone would call out the answer before Jolene even had the chance to figure out it was her brother's voice.

Jolene began drawing the circles. She drew one, and then a second that was positioned on top of the first—they overlapped a little, but it was pretty accurate for being blindfolded. She started to draw the third circle, but then she stopped, holding her pencil completely still.

My heart raced because I knew she had figured something out.

"Wes?" she asked.

"Yeah?" Wes answered.

"Okay, for a second... you sounded like..."

Slowly, Jolene continued drawing the third circle. She had stopped and started on this one, so it was completely in the wrong place, and we all smiled at each other at the sight of it being several inches from the others.

"Now, I'm going to help you find the right spot, and when we get there, I want you to draw a little line, about an inch long."

"That is not Wes," she said. "Who's giving me clues?"

"Who do you think it is?" I asked.

"It sounds exactly like my brother. Who is it? Liam? Uncle Gray?"

"What if it *is* your brother?" Luke asked.

Jolene was still for a second, and then, all at once, she gasped and spun around on her stool, ripping her blindfold off.

I couldn't stop myself from laughing as I watched them. I felt like I wanted to laugh and cry at the same time. She stared straight at her brother in total amazement before shooting off of her stool to hug him.

"What in the world are you doing here?" she squealed. "I can't believe it!"

She squeezed him tightly before pulling back to regard him at arm's length. She glanced around at all of us who were standing around, watching them.

"Did you know about this?" she asked, looking straight at Wes.

He shook his head, holding his hands up innocently.

"He had no idea," I said.

"What are you doing here?" she asked. "Is everything okay? Are Mom and Dad—"

"Everything's fine," Luke said with a broad smile.

He reached for me, pulling me toward him.

My heart hammered in my chest as I took those steps, coming to stand right next to Luke and directly in front of Jolene. He put his arm around me protectively.

"I came here for Ivy," he said.

I honestly expected her to squeal with delight and reach out to embrace us, but to my horror, the opposite happened.

Her smile faded and her face became a mask of confusion and maybe even distress. She hadn't even said a thing and, already, I felt like I couldn't breathe. Everyone was silent, watching us.

"What?" she asked, still looking dumfounded.

"Ivy," he said calmly. "She and I are… well, we're in love, Jo. We love each other."

He sounded way more composed than I felt.

Dread and panic washed over me because of the disgruntled look on her face.

"No," she said, shaking her head a little and staring at us. "You must be joking."

"I thought you'd be happy," Luke said.

"Are you guys playing a joke on me or something?" She looked around with a little smile like she thought she might be on a hidden camera show. Then her smile fell as she regarded us again. She was stunned, not happy at all. "Please tell me you're joking." she said.

"Babe, calm down," Wes said in a comforting tone.

My mom stepped forward. "Luke came in last week to see Ivy. They thought they would surprise you."

"Well, they sure did surprise me," Jolene said seriously with wide eyes. She shook her head in dismay as she continued to look at us. I saw her eyes go to the place where Luke's hand was wrapped around my shoulder, and she stared at us as if she was sickened by the sight of us together.

My heart was broken.

I was shocked and humiliated.

I was speechless. I didn't know what to do or say. Never, in a million years, would I have anticipated her reacting this way.

"I can't believe you're serious," she said, looking straight at Luke.

She looked at me.

I wanted to cry.

I wanted to disappear into thin air.

"You better stop," Luke said. "She's gonna think you're actually serious."

"I'm totally not serious," Jolene said, looking at me with a straight face. I felt like I was dreaming as her scowl slowly turned to a little smirk.

My stomach churned and my heart pounded.

I felt the blood leave my face. *What was going on?* I turned to stare up at Luke who glanced at me with a little grin. He held me tightly, which was a good thing, because I was weak in the knees.

Luke smiled and leaned down to kiss my cheek. "Jolene's not the one being surprised here," he said.

"She's not?" I asked weakly.

I glanced around, noticing everyone's eyes on me. They were all smiling. A couple of them—Shug and my mom were looking like they wanted to cry. Even the babies were standing around, watching. Uncle Gray had out his phone and was videoing. It was completely surreal.

There were so many people staring at me that it took a few seconds for my eyes to fall on them. I had to do a double take. Ben and Ginger Wright were standing at the edge of the crowd. They were holding onto each other and Ginger was staring at me expectantly with her hands clasped in front of her face like she, too, was about to cry.

"What, wh… what are y'all…" I looked at Luke again. "Your parents," I said. "Is that your parents?"

He nodded, and I felt Jolene reach out to hug me. She took me into her arms. "I'm so sorry," she said, laughing a little. "I had to mess with you a little. I love you, Ivy, and I couldn't be happier that you love my brother."

I hugged her back. I didn't fully understand what was going on, but I was so very relieved to see a smile on her face.

"I couldn't resist teasing you a little when Luke told us your big plan," she said.

I turned around so that I could face Luke. "You told them my plan?" I asked.

"I had to," he said. "Because I had a plan of my own."

"You did?"

"He does," Jolene said proudly as she stepped back to sit on her stool.

"A big one," my mom said.

Again, I glanced around, and could see that most of the women in the room had their hands in front of their faces like they were about to cry or were already crying. Daniel must have noticed it as well because I heard him say, "We might need a box of tissues over here," causing everyone to laugh.

"Are your mom and dad really here?" I asked Luke. I truly thought I might be seeing things.

He nodded. "They flew in this afternoon."

I glanced at them, and Ginger smiled and waved at me. I waved back, although it was probably somewhat stiff since I was still stunned.

"I'm only going to do this one time in my whole life," Luke said. "So, I wanted to do it right."

"Amen to that!" my dad said.

And then it happened.

Right there in front of God and everybody, Luke went to his knees. Not one knee, like you see in the movies, but both of them. He got on both of his knees, holding onto me by gripping onto my pants and staring straight up at me. He was so tall, that even on his knees, his face was almost at my chest.

Hot tears sprang to my eyes as I realized what he was doing. I could hear people around me whimpering and sniffling, which made me cry even more. I held onto Luke's arm, feeling like if I didn't, I might fall over.

"Ivy Bishop, I love you more than any man has ever loved any woman, ever."

I smiled at him, and he smiled back.

Various noises were coming from the onlookers, but our eyes were trained on each other. I stared straight at him feeling an undeniable sense of comfort in the midst of this whirlwind of emotions.

"Please, please, my sweet, precious, beautiful Ivy, would you please marry me?"

"Oh, Luke, yes! Oh my gosh, of course, yes, yes, yes."

My face crumpled as I collapsed into his arms. He caught me and held me there while everyone cheered and clapped. There was so much noise and movement that I didn't even know how we got to our feet.

One second, we were on our knees, then we on our feet, and then, just like that, my feet were no longer touching the floor. Luke lifted me by the waist, and I held his face in my hands as I kissed him over and over again. People were clapping, whistling, cheering, crying, talking, and patting us on our backs. It was the most beautiful chaos I had ever experienced.

"Don't forget the ring!" someone yelled out.

"Oh yeah," Luke said. (kiss) "There's a (kiss) ring in my (kiss) pocket."

I smiled, stealing a quick glance at his gorgeous mouth as he smiled back. "I'll get it later," I said before kissing him again.

Epilogue

It was difficult to watch Luke get on an airplane to go back to London. I knew in my heart that a three-month separation wasn't a big deal, but I had grown undeniably accustomed to having him around.

I didn't have any plans to go to London during that time, but at a little over the half-way point (in early May) I broke down and booked a trip. I was non-stop back home with wrapping up the school year at the nonprofit and getting prepped for summer programs. Making sure the contractors focused on finishing the house was a job in itself, but I got desperate and cleared my schedule for three days so I could go to London to see him.

That trip was short, but it was just the boost I needed. Seeing Luke was like a breath of fresh air. It motivated me to work even harder to prepare myself and our home for his arrival.

My contractor had crews at the house around the clock, and my family also helped tremendously. Between my parents, siblings, cousins, and aunts and uncles, I had lots of help. I also received a lot of really nice hand-me-down furniture that made the house feel comfortable and warm right from the start. My aunt Rhonda was an expert gardener, and she put my dad and brothers to work, planting and seeding. I couldn't believe how quickly it all came together. It turned out even better than I pictured.

I moved in five days before Luke's arrival. I had planned on spending my first night there with Luke, but the house was finished early, and I loved it so much that I couldn't resist moving in once it was done.

Shug and Doozy gave us their gigantic four-poster bed for the master bedroom. She said it was because she wanted to get something new, but I knew she just wanted to give me her old one. It was made of cherry wood with thick, ornate posts. I had always loved that bed. I looked forward to spending the night at Shug and Doozy's because I loved sleeping in that bed—it made me feel like a princess. And now it was mine. Ours. She gave us the frame and dresser and even bought us a new memory foam mattress for it.

My mom and dad supplied the bedding—a beautiful, fluffy, light grey comforter with matching sheets and lots of throw pillows. It was the most luxurious sleeping situation I could ever imagine.

Luke flew in the evening before the wedding. We both knew we were cutting it close with choosing to book his flight that close to the wedding, especially with possible flight delays or cancelations, but that's just the way it had to be. If Luke and I would have had it our way, we would have planned the wedding the instant he stepped off the plane, so it was already a stretch to give ourselves the one-day buffer.

I didn't see him at all the evening he flew in. I hadn't seen him since my trip to London, which was five weeks ago. He was staying at my parents' house, and knowing he was there was torture for me, but I kept myself away. My whole family knew we were waiting until the wedding, so they all chipped in with helping us stay away from each other.

Luke's parents had flown in with him, and they came to our new house the evening before the wedding, but they made Luke stay behind. Mr. Wright had an extensive collection of fine art, and he brought three amazing paintings for us. I knew they were coming. I had been given their dimensions and had prepared places on the wall for them, so when he and Ginger came over, we made quick work of hanging them up. The Wrights were happy with how the paintings looked in our new home, and I was ever so grateful for the gorgeous gifts. I was sad, however, that they left Luke behind when they came. I was desperate to see him.

My brothers and their families were at my parents' house, so they kept him occupied. I could not believe he was so close to me and we weren't seeing each other. *Whose crazy idea was this, anyway? Okay, so it was mine, but what was I thinking?* I really regretted saying I didn't want to see him before the wedding, and I did my best to try to talk everyone into letting me change my mind, but they assured me that these short hours would fly by and I would live through the torture.

I tried my best to make it, I really did, but at midnight, the temptation proved to be too much. I sent him a text.

Me: "I can't do it."

Luke: "Can't do what?"

Me: "Wait."

Luke: "Me neither. I hate this."

Me: "Come to my window."

Luke: "I thought you'd never ask. Be there in five minutes."

Me: "You know which one?"

Luke: "Yes. Five minutes."

I was absolutely giddy.

I sprang off of the bed and went to the bathroom to run a toothbrush over my teeth. I had already brushed my teeth, but one more time couldn't hurt. I literally laughed with nerves and excitement as I did my best to spiffy my pajama-clad self up in those minutes while he was on his way.

I had the window open and was kneeling down beside it by the time he got there. There was a sheer curtain hanging, and I left that closed so that he couldn't see inside. I peeked around the side of it and could see his silhouette approaching in the distance. I was absolutely breathless with anticipation. I stayed there, near the window, unable to see anything as I not-so-patiently waited the remaining seconds.

"Pssst," I heard him say once he walked up to the window.

I pulled back the curtain, peeking out shyly. It was dark out, so it took us a second to find each other.

"Ohhh, baby girl," he said with a sigh. He reached out and grabbed my face, kissing me gently over and over again. All over my cheeks, he placed kiss after kiss.

I was moved by the relief he expressed.

He was as desperate for me as I was for him, and the sight and feel of it moved me to tears. There was nothing I could do to stop tears of relief and joy from rolling onto my cheeks as he kissed me. He pulled back and stared at me with a look of concern when he realized I was crying.

"Are you okay?" he asked softly.

I nodded. "I just missed you," I said. "I'm so happy you're here."

He smiled and kissed me again, three more times. These were on the lips and they were hotter and more branding than the ones that came before.

"I love you like crazy, my Ivy-girl."

"I love you, too," I said, still crying even though I tried not to.

"I can't wait to marry you tomorrow," he said.

"Me neither. I can't wait."

He kissed me again. He looked me straight in the eyes. "It's gonna be perfect," he said. "And then, when it's over, I won't have to sneak up to your window anymore. I can go right inside and get in that bed with you."

I nodded. "I've been thinking about it so much that I dream about it."

He gave me one last kiss on the lips before letting go of my face. He smiled as he took a step back. "By the way, why am I at your window? Why couldn't you just meet me at the front door?"

I let out a little laugh through the tears. "I don't know. Maybe it's fun to sneak around even if nobody's here to catch us."

He nodded. "It was fun."

"You say 'was' like it's over," I said.

"It is over, baby girl."

He straightened, touching my cheek with the side of his finger in a gesture of goodbye. "I have to go before I climb in through this window."

I smiled and nodded. "I love you," I called, as he turned to leave.

"I love you too," he said from over his shoulder as he retreated into the darkness.

I closed the window and went to bed with a grin on my face.

***

The wedding was at noon followed by a reception where we served lunch.

It turned out to be a larger wedding than I anticipated, but during the planning, my dad kept using Luke's words from when he proposed.

I'd say, *"No, we don't need to do that,"* or *"We don't need to invite them,"* and he'd say, "Ivy, you're only gonna do this one time in your whole life."

Maybe it had something to do with the fact that I was his only daughter or that Luke didn't have any family or friends in Memphis, but it seemed like my dad wanted to invite the whole town. I seriously think he invited everyone who worked for Bishop Motorcycles, simply because he didn't know where to draw the line and didn't want to hurt anyone's feelings.

Just under three hundred people showed up for the event. Luke had a few from London and several others from different parts of the U.S., but the guest list was, by in large, people my dad insisted on inviting. Not that I was in any position to complain. He only did it because he was proud of me and wanted everyone to be there to witness my big day.

I couldn't have been more pleased with the way things turned out. We had an outdoor wedding on some beautiful riverside property that Owen and Darcy owned on the outskirts of town. We rented tents and hired catering and a band, and by the time it was all said and done, it was the party of the year.

Even the kiddos were dressed formally for the occasion. Kip was the ring bearer and little Cora was the flower girl. I had six bridesmaids standing up there with me—Shelby, Courtney, Darcy, Jolene, Taylor, and a good friend of mine named Katie who now worked with me. Luke had six groomsmen, my three brothers, my cousin, Liam, and two of his good friends from London. Luke and I were so easy-going about it that we honestly didn't care who was standing up there with us or what they were wearing. My mom and the wedding planner took care of choosing everything, and Taylor took care of the clothing. They all just ran things past me to make sure I was satisfied (which I always was since they did an amazing job).

Grandpa Jacob performed a short, sweet ceremony, after which we ate, drank, talked, laughed, and danced until late in the afternoon.

Just in case you were wondering, Britney was in attendance. Our friendship had not been restored to the level it was before the incident, but I had long since forgiven her. And, honestly, I was grateful for whatever had happened to bring Luke and me together, no matter how painful it was at the time. She and her boyfriend stayed for the ceremony, and afterward, she hugged me and thanked me for inviting them. She wished us all the best before heading home. I told her they were welcome to stay for the reception, but she graciously declined, thanking me again for the invitation. I felt closure, and I was thankful that I had thought to add her to the guest list. To me, it was a nice addition to an already perfect day.

A few speeches were given during the course of the reception, but at around 4pm when things were winding down, my father got everyone's attention.

He gave a sentimental, heartfelt speech about me being his baby girl. Just about everyone, including my father himself, was moved to tears.

My favorite part, however, came after his speech. He had talked about his respect for Luke and his genuine excitement about Luke being a part of the Bishop Motorcycle legacy. He explained how Luke's genius design won their hearts before they ever knew Luke had won my heart. He gave a brief description of the designs Luke had submitted, and then he casually said, "You know what? It's too hard for me to explain how good they were, I'll just let y'all see for yourself."

Right after he said that, he motioned to someone in the distance, and then we heard the rumbling sound of engines revving to life. We all turned in shock and amazement as two of the guys from the shop rode up on Luke's motorcycles, circling around the crowd and stopping in front of everybody.

Once they parked and killed the engines, my dad explained that these models would not be out until the following winter but that these beautiful prototypes were wedding gifts to Luke and me.

That was just too much for me. I knew just how excited Luke was to see his designs come to life. He wasn't an overly-emotional guy, but I could see how overwhelmed he was as he walked up to the bikes. They were truly awe-inspiring, and I cried like a baby watching him walk around them, touching

216

things and checking them out. I don't know if there was a time I had ever been so proud.

The remainder of the reception passed in a blur.

Most of our guests were motorcycle lovers, so they were truly interested in checking out the bikes and asking questions about them. We expected to drive off in the back of a rented classic limo, but it was a no-brainer, once those bikes arrived, that we would ride off into the sunset on them instead.

We didn't go to a hotel or to the airport. We went straight to our house—the place I'd been preparing for him. Luke and I both liked to travel, and we planned on traveling soon and often, but our honeymoon was going to be held right here in this house. For the next three days, we were not to be bothered. The fridge and pantry were stocked, and we weren't planning on leaving the premises or talking to anyone else. Seventy-two hours of Luke and Ivy only, and I already felt like it wouldn't be enough.

We parked the bikes in the garage, staring at them one last time before heading into the house. Luke threw me over his shoulder on the way inside, saying he needed to fulfill some sort of tradition about crossing the threshold.

He set me to my feet, once we made it in the door, and we straightened, wrapping our arms around each other and staring straight into each other's eyes.

"What do you think about the house?" I asked, still locking eyes with him.

"What house?" he said.

I smiled. "I guess you've got time to check it out later," I said.

"I can see that it's nice out of the corner of my eye," he said, still staring straight at me. His hungry eyes roamed over my face, stopping at my mouth. "I'm sure it's fine," he said.

I smiled. "I guess you don't want to see the bedroom, then," I said, teasing him.

And before I knew it, I was tossed over his shoulder again. He was so big, and the movement was so sudden that I squealed. He basically ran through the house, causing me to giggle and squirm as he held me securely. I landed in the middle of my soft, perfect princess bed and smiled at my sweet, handsome prince.

"I love your mouth," I said unable to stop myself from being anything but honest as I stared at his irresistible smile.

"Good, because it loves you," he said.

He was wearing a mischievous grin as he crawled onto the bed with me. Anticipation coursed through my body, causing me to squirm. He kissed me, and what followed that kiss was raw and wonderful. I was Mrs. Ivy Wright, and that was exactly who I was supposed to be.

The End

Post Epilogue Fun Facts:
(Updates on the Bishop clan and those they love.)

Luke and Ivy:

Luke's motorcycles (the Ace LT and Ace MT) were a big hit, just like Doozy knew they would be. They were released the following season and received rave reviews on their sleek styling and smooth riding. Luke easily stepped into a role of leadership at Bishop Motorcycles—designing and helping run the company alongside his in-laws. It was the job he had been created for.

Luke and Jolene's father applied for a job at Vanderbilt in Nashville. Only months after Luke and Ivy's wedding, he and Ginger moved back to the U.S. and had been residing in Nashville ever since. Everyone enjoyed having them closer.

There was a real need in Memphis for the services Ivy's nonprofit provided, and it grew quickly. Soon, she had more students than she could handle. The musicians in the family (Shug, Courtney, and Wes) put on a fund-raising concert at Courtney's center. It turned out to be a big deal. They recorded a live album during the event, and the proceeds from it all helped Ivy hire more teachers and purchase a larger facility. Memphis Learning Center moved to a building that was three times the size of the original one. Ivy even established a simple garage set-up where Luke and Owen taught shop classes twice a week.

Luke and Ivy had three beautiful girls before she gave birth to a son. They welcomed Lily, Addison, Alice, and then finally a little boy came along. Ivy got more patient as the years passed. They didn't have an ultrasound to find out whether the fourth baby was a boy or a girl, and they didn't tell anyone the names they were considering. Ivy's father was obviously thrilled when they named him Jesse.

Wes and Jolene:
Wes continued making music and recording albums. He went on tour several months of each year to support his albums and connect with his fans. He wasn't a sell-out-arenas type of artist like Courtney had been, but he had a loyal following and he made a good living doing something he loved.

Jolene continued to work in graphic design. Between all of the family businesses, she had more than enough design work to keep her busy. She and Luke also worked with Uncle Gray, giving knife throwing classes at Alpha. Wes and Jolene had two handsome sons, Ethan and Benjamin.

Shelby and Isaac:
For a while, Isaac continued to do architecture all around the country. He had plenty of business in Memphis, but he and Shelby both enjoyed traveling. Once their two children, Cora and Oliver, were old enough to start school, Isaac started taking less out-of-town work. He reserved those jobs for the

summer when he could bring the whole family along.

He and Shelby built a really beautiful, unique, home on some land near Courtney and Daniel. He took great care in designing the house and pulled out all the stops with his unorthodox architecture. It was stunning. It boasted a grand spiral staircase and a massive metal slide that ran along the side of the house from a second-story balcony to the ground below. Their house was always a hit for family gatherings.

Liam and Taylor:

Liam continued working for his father's company, Alpha Security. He, too, had to travel some, but he was usually only out of town for a few days at a time, so generally, Taylor didn't travel with him. She was extremely busy running her bespoke tailoring business, anyway. Taylor Made provided suits for Memphis's most discerning suit connoisseurs. Her downtown storefront had a vintage feel that added charm and elegance to the cityscape. Taylor's shop became a Memphis tradition that seemed like it had always been there.

In addition to running her business, she somehow managed to also be a caring attentive mother. She and Liam raised three gorgeous boys. Mack, Caleb, and Eli. Little Eli was a heartbreaker from day one, inheriting his mother's thick black hair and ice-blue eyes.

Also, on a side note, Vera and Victor (the Basset Hounds) had a litter of six puppies, one of which Liam and Taylor kept. One went to Ivy and Luke, one to Ben and Ginger in Nashville, and another to Uncle Max and Aunt Betty. The remaining two were adopted by employees at Bishop.

Owen and Darcy:
Owen and Darcy basically owned half of Memphis. Darcy had fallen heir to her father's properties and fortune, which were extensive. Managing their holdings proved to be a full-time job, and Darcy, being a determined steward, became a savvy landlord and property manager. With hard work and sound financial advice, she turned their fortune into an even greater fortune. They were extremely generous. They used their position of wealth for good, and God blessed them for it.

Owen continued to work at Bishop Motorcycles, but only because he loved it and wanted to be there. When the twins, Colin and Cole, were three years old, Darcy gave birth to a third son. They called him Reid.

Courtney and Daniel:
Courtney's art center was one of Memphis's most beloved institutions. She set it in motion, and she spent some time there, but it was a huge undertaking that was run by the capable people she put in charge. Five years after she had Kip and Eden, she came out

of musical retirement just along enough to record an album and go on tour. She spent six months on a world tour and enjoyed every moment of it, knowing she would take at least another five years off afterward.

Daniel quit work at Alpha. He still went to the facility to work out and keep in touch with the guys, but he focused his efforts on maintaining their family property, which could now be considered a farm. He and Courtney didn't set out to own a farm, but they both enjoyed eating wholesome, organic foods. Little by little, they became somewhat self-sustained. They had a huge garden with sheep and chickens, and they now yielded enough crops to provide for other members of the family. After her come-back tour, Courtney gave birth to two more boys, Alec and Michael. They had a total of four children, three boys and a girl. Kip, Eden, Alec, and Michael.

Gray and Jane:

Gray found pleasure and fulfillment as the owner of Alpha Security. They trained elite-level bodyguards, equipping them for work protecting some of the most important people in the world. He took good men and made them into better ones through his two-year program. It was good, clean fun for Gray, and he got to make a great living while he was at it.

Jane was a homemaker, but she spent a lot of time at Alpha. She took pleasure in setting a tone of positivity in her home and at their business. Like her mother, she always had a song in her heart and on her lips. Life was good at the Kennedy house. Gray and Jane had two children, Shelby and Liam, and five grandchildren, Cora, Oliver, Mack, Caleb, and Eli.

Jesse and Rose:
Bishop Motorcycle Company was their home away from home. Rose worked in marketing and accounting while Jesse helped his father run the family business. They both loved the company and had devoted their life's work to insuring its success. Jesse truly enjoyed working on bikes, and even if he had a long day in the office, he would make time at the end of it to get his hands greasy in the garage.

Jesse and Rose were still as in love today as they were the day they got married. They could often be found sitting in the same chair, with Rose curled up on her husband's lap. They had four children, Daniel, Owen, Wes, and Ivy, and thirteen grandchildren, Kip, Eden, Alec, Michael, Colin, Cole, Reid, Ethan, Benjamin, Lily, Addison, Alice, and Jesse.

Ivy and Michael (Shug and Doozy):
What can I say? Shug and Doozy really had it figured out. They had an unbelievably full life, surrounded by their family. They'd be the first to

admit that finding happiness in life isn't really as complicated as it might seem.

They believed in some basic truths like honesty, loyalty, communication, perseverance, being content with what you have, and enjoying life's simple pleasures. They would tell you that the secret to happiness is pretty simple, really. They'd say you ought to love the Lord your God with all your heart, soul and strength, and love your neighbor as yourself. With a true understanding of that basic principle, everything else falls into place.

They had been through a lot of life's ups and downs together, but they, too, were still just as infatuated with each other as they were the day they met. Shug still got butterflies when Doozy smiled just the right way. They had two children, Jesse and Jane, six grandchildren, Daniel, Owen, Wes, Ivy, Shelby, and Liam, and eighteen great-grandchildren, Kip, Eden, Alec, Michael, Colin, Cole, Reid, Ethan, Benjamin, Lily, Addison, Alice, Jesse, Cora, Oliver, Mack, Caleb, and blue-eyed Eli.

Thank you, from the bottom of my heart, for reading the Bishop Family series. I hope you have enjoyed getting to know this family as much as I have enjoyed sharing them.

~Brooke

Thanks to my team ~
Chris, Coda, Jan, and Glenda

Made in the USA
Middletown, DE
02 August 2021